THE FRIGHT OF HER LIFE

I heard a new sound. Not the wind and the rain. Not the crash of thunder. Not the cat. Just a small voice, crying out somewhere above me.

A human voice, a little girl's, crying out in a house that was empty except for the cat and me.

A shiver rippled through me. I had to get out of here!

I started for the door and then stopped.

"What are you so afraid of, Nine?" I whispered to myself. "You know who that voice belongs to. It's just a little kid—a lonely little girl, crying in her bed."

All right—so it was a dead kid. She was still lonely.

Taking a deep breath, I headed for the stairs—and the waiting ghost.

OTHER DELL YEARLING BOOKS
YOU WILL ENJOY

DELL YEARLING BOOKS are designed especially to entertain and enlighten young people. Patricia Reilly Giff, consultant to this series, received her bachelor's degree from Marymount College and a master's degree in history from St. John's University. She holds a Professional Diploma in Reading and a Doctorate of Humane Letters from Hofstra University. She was a teacher and reading consultant for many years, and is the author of numerous books for young readers.

THE GHOST
IN THE BIG BRASS BED

BRUCE COVILLE

A Dell Yearling Book

For Danelle,
who, like Alida, had to wait

Published by
Dell Yearling
an imprint of
Random House Children's Books
a division of Random House, Inc.
New York

Visit us on the Web! www.randomhouse.com/kids

Educators and librarians, for a variety of teaching tools,
visit us at www.randomhouse.com/teachers

ISBN: 0-553-15827-9

Reprinted by arrangement with Bantam Books

Printed in the United States of America

First Dell Yearling Edition July 2001

20 19 18

OPM

CONTENTS

CHAPTER ONE

The Caffeine Poster Child

You could say I met the ghost of Cornelius Fletcher because of my father's three-dollar coffee maker.

My dad had just bought the coffee maker at a garage sale. Personally I thought this was a dumb idea; in my opinion, drinking coffee is a lot like sucking old sweat socks.

My father, however, was very pleased with himself. "Three dollars," he said with a chuckle as we started walking home along Westcott Street. "I can't believe she sold it to me for only three dollars!"

"*I* can't believe you *bought* it," I replied.

"That, my little pookanilly, is because you have underdeveloped taste buds."

My search for a killer response was interrupted by someone shouting, "Henry! Henry Tanleven! What are you doing, walking down Westcott Street with a coffee maker under your arm?"

1

We turned to our right. "Norma Bliss!" my dad exclaimed. "What are *you* doing here?"

"I live here—as of two months ago."

"Come on," my father whispered to me. "You'll enjoy this."

I followed him up the steps of a pale green house. The woman who had called out to us was very pretty. She had skin the color of chocolate, huge eyes, and a smile like a sunrise over a lake. Her voice was deep and raspy. She was sitting on a porch swing. Near the swing stood a round white table. On the table sat a big cup of coffee and a coffee maker.

As we stepped onto the porch, she said, "To tell you the truth, Henry, it was your coffee maker that got my attention. I saw you with that machine, and I said to myself, 'Norma, there goes *your* kind of man.' Then I realized it was you!"

She threw back her head and laughed. It was a wonderful laugh. Even so, I was not totally amused. The last thing I needed right now was another woman going after my father. Ever since my mother left, I've had this problem with him.

Dad is pretty bright about most things. But when it comes to women, he needs a lot of help. Of course, at the moment he was focused on his coffee maker. Patting it fondly, he gave me a triumphant smirk, then turned back to his friend.

"Norma, I'd like you to meet my daughter, Nine."

"Nine?" asked Norma, managing to lower her chin and raise an eyebrow at the same time.

"It's really Nina," I said. "But everyone calls me Nine, because of my last name."

Norma thought for a second, then grinned. "Nine Tan-Leven!" she said. "I like that!"

A point in her favor. Most adults say, "Isn't that *cute*?", which makes me want to barf.

"Norma's an antique dealer," my dad said.

"Bliss in Brass," she said proudly, pointing to the red pickup truck that sat in her driveway. The store name was painted on the door, inside an oval design. "Actually, I handle a lot of wooden stuff, too, but 'A Broad and Her Boards' just didn't have the same ring."

"Nine's kind of interested in antiques."

That was my father's idea of a joke. What he meant was that I'm interested in ghosts. I suppose you *could* call them antiques, but it seems to me that's really stretching things.

I didn't start out to be a ghost specialist. Oh, I liked ghost stories as much as any other kid I've ever met. But it wasn't until my best friend Chris Gurley and I started running into the real thing that I began to take them seriously.

Our first experience was with the Woman in White, the ghost who haunted the Grand Theater. We figured one ghost could happen to anyone. But after we met Captain Jonathan Gray, the ghost of the Quackadoodle Inn, Chris and I began to wonder if we had some kind of special spirit-spotting ability.

Norma was looking at me with new interest. "Do you think you might want a job?"

"What kind of a job?"

"I need an extra hand at the shop. Nothing major—I've already got an assistant. What I'm looking for is someone who likes antiques but doesn't need work on a regular basis. Sounds like you might fill the bill."

"But I'm only eleven," I said, ignoring the fact that we had been talking about different kinds of antiques anyway.

"That's okay," said Norma. "I'm not prejudiced."

Which is how I ended up with a part-time job at Bliss in Brass—and how I met my next ghost.

"You are *so-o-o-o* lucky," Chris said when I called to tell her about the job. "First the book, now this."

Chris had been a little jealous ever since this editor named Mona Curtis asked me to write a book about our first adventure. Mona asked *me* to write the book because my father showed her the pages of my journal where I talked about meeting the Woman in White.

I was pretty mad when he did that without asking me. But when I learned I might get to write a book because of it, I had a hard time staying angry.

Actually, Chris wasn't that upset about the book. After all, she doesn't keep a journal, and she doesn't particularly want to be a writer. So she says it's okay, as long as I tell everyone how beautiful and smart she is. (She's going to kill me when she reads this.)

Now with something like that going on, you wouldn't think I'd need a part-time job. But I didn't have a contract yet. Mona wanted me to write several chapters first. And my dad had already informed me that if I *did* make anything on the book, most of it was getting put away for college. So earning a little extra money didn't seem like a bad idea.

Any jealousy Chris had about the job vanished when I told her Norma's shop was less than ten blocks from her house.

"All right!" she shouted, nearly breaking my eardrum.

The reason this was so exciting is that Chris and I live on different sides of town and go to different schools—which makes it a big problem for us to get together. I was even happier about the job at Norma's when my father told me I could spend the night with Chris whenever I worked there. Of course, it had to be all right with Chris's parents.

Every time the phone rang that week, I jumped for it, hoping it would be Norma asking me to work. But it wasn't until Thursday that I picked up the receiver and heard a gravelly voice ask, "So, Nine—are you working for me Saturday, or not?"

"Working!" I cried, trying to keep from shouting with delight.

Saturday morning I walked to Norma's house. She was waiting in her red pickup. A terrifying ten minutes later we pulled up in front of Bliss in Brass. It *should* have been a fifteen-minute ride, but Norma drives the way she does everything else: fast!

I was still thinking how glad I was to be in one piece when Norma said, "Are you getting out, or are you going to sit there all day?" I blinked when I realized she was already out of the truck and standing next to my window.

Bliss in Brass was an old red building nestled at the end of a row of houses. I think it had been a house once itself. A low stone wall ran along the edge of the lawn, which was about three feet higher than the sidewalk. In front of the shop stood a wooden sign, carved with the same design that was painted on the side of Norma's truck.

Through the picture window to the left of the door I could see beautiful old dressers, beds, and mirrors. The inside of the shop was even better— crowded, but not *too* crowded, and arranged so that each thing you looked at seemed to lead you on to the next. Old-fashioned quilts and lots of pillows made the shop feel cozy and homey.

The shop even smelled good, as if Norma had tucked spices into the corners.

Of course, it also smelled like coffee. (How can something smell so good and taste so gross?)

Norma sniffed the air as we walked in. "Ahh," she said happily. "It's working!"

I followed her to the back of the shop, where I saw a large coffee maker. Hot coffee was dripping into the glass pot.

Norma flashed me a huge grin. "I bought this yesterday. It has an automatic timer. Now I can have fresh coffee as soon as I get here. Want some?"

I made a face. "I never touch the stuff."

Norma rolled her eyes. "I couldn't live without it. I used to have a boyfriend who called me the Caffeine Poster Child."

She poured herself a cup, and we got to work. The first thing I had to do was dust. Gag. I *hate* dusting! Except somehow doing it here wasn't as annoying as doing it at home.

Besides, here I was getting paid for it.

I had been working for about ten minutes when the bell over the door rang. Looking up, I saw an elderly woman enter the shop.

She was probably as old as half the things in the store; her hair was white as baby powder, and her pale skin looked like a piece of paper that's been wrinkled up, then smoothed out again. She

Bruce Coville

had to lean on a cane to walk, and as she hobbled toward me I got the feeling that if I sneezed too hard, I might knock her down.

She stopped in front of me, put her hand on the dresser I was dusting, and burst into tears.

CHAPTER TWO

Phoebe Watson

What are you supposed to do when an old lady stands in front of you and starts to cry? Part of me was disgusted; I think adults should have more self-control. Part of me was scared; what if she was crazy? Part of me just wanted to hug her and say, "There, there, it'll be all right."

Finally I put down my dust rag and asked, "Can I help you?"

The old lady fumbled in her purse for a tissue. "I'm sorry," she said, dabbing at her eyes. "That wasn't fair to you. It's just that this dresser used to be in my house. Seeing it here makes me sad." Still sniffing a little, she ran her fingers over the area I had been dusting.

Her answer only raised more questions, such as: What was the dresser doing *here*? Had someone stolen it? Had the woman sold it to Norma? And if she missed it so much, why didn't she just buy it back?

Before I could decide which to ask first, Norma came sailing across the shop, shouting, "Fee-bee!" (Actually, she was shouting, "Phoebe!"—but I didn't know how to spell it until I saw it written down later.)

Taking the woman by the arm, Norma asked, "How *are* you?"

Phoebe smiled, but her eyes looked as sad as ever. "Not so good," she said softly.

Norma took her hand. "Well, you just come over here and tell Norma all about it," she said, tugging Phoebe toward the coffee area. The old woman went along quietly.

My curiosity was killing me. I was still trying to figure out some way to go listen to them when the bell at the front of the shop tinkled again and Chris Gurley walked in.

"What are *you* doing here?" I yelled.

"I came to look around," Chris said, surprised.

Suddenly I realized how rude I must have sounded. It was just that I was afraid Norma would be upset with me for having friends in the shop when I was supposed to be working.

"Here to case the joint, huh?" I said, smiling.

"You've been watching too many old movies," replied Chris. "They're affecting your vocabulary."

But she said it with a smile, too. Things were okay.

A few minutes later Norma and Phoebe joined us. Norma was holding Phoebe's arm, which meant that she had to walk at the same slow pace as the old lady. It probably drove her nuts to move that way, but she managed to smile anyway.

"Introduction time!" she said, waving her free hand. "Phoebe, this young lady is my new assistant, Nina Tanleven. You can call her Nine. Nine, this is Phoebe Watson."

"Pleased to meet you, Ms. Watson," I said.

"I'd prefer you to call me Phoebe," she said, putting out her hand for me to shake. I took it. Her skin was smooth and soft.

I introduced Chris and explained that I would be going to her house when I was done working.

"Whoo, child," said Norma. "Are you the one Henry was telling me about—the one Nine's been solving mysteries with? Honey, I don't know how the two of you stand it! When I'm alone in this shop at night, it's all I can do to walk from one end of this room to the other. If I ever saw a ghost in here, I wouldn't *bother* opening the door; I'd go through the glass and pick up the pieces later!"

"Have you girls really seen a ghost?" Phoebe asked.

"Several," Chris said, and grinned.

"How interesting. I've always been fascinated by ghosts."

"Lord, Phoebe, don't talk like that!" Norma rolled her eyes. "I don't want to see a ghost. I don't want to hear a ghost. I don't even want to know about a ghost!"

Phoebe looked troubled. Before I could figure out a way to ask why, Norma said, "Phoebe's selling me an old wardrobe. I'm going over to her house to pick it up after we close this afternoon. If you have time, Nine, I'd like you to come along." She paused, then added, "You can come, too, Chris, if you want."

"All right!" shouted Chris. Then she raised her eyebrows and slapped her hand over her mouth.

I watched through the shop window as Phoebe drove away. Her car was even older than my father's, and when she hunched down behind the steering wheel, she could barely see over the dashboard. I had a feeling that riding with her might be even scarier than riding with Norma!

I went back to my dusting while Chris called her mother to see if it was all right if she made the trip. She flashed me the OK sign from the phone. We were all set!

When some customers wandered into the store, Chris decided to go home. "I don't want Norma to think I'm getting in the way," she whispered just before she left.

I nodded. "See you later."

She showed up again just as we were closing the shop.

"Oh, there you are!" Norma said happily. "I was starting to worry that you had forgotten us."

"Not a chance!"

I decided not to mention the fact that Chris's father had once threatened to have her name legally changed to Chris "Late Again" Gurley.

"Phoebe lives only a mile or two from Westcott Street, so we'll be driving back through our own neighborhood," Norma told me, as she locked the door of the shop. "Kind of a sad old lady," she continued as the three of us climbed into the truck. "She must have sold more than half her furniture over the last few years."

"How come?" Chris asked.

"Too many expenses, not enough income," said Norma as she pulled out of the driveway and roared up the street. "Happens to a lot of older people." She took a swig of coffee from her travel cup, then stuck it back on the dashboard.

"I thought the government took care of people like that," I said.

Norma snorted so hard that she nearly blew coffee through her nose. "Honey, that government 'safety net' has more holes than a pair of cheap panty hose at the end of a bad day."

A car honked as we cut into the right lane. We hit the highway and headed for our neighborhood, which is known as the university section, because it's close to Syracuse University.

"Look!" Chris exclaimed when we reached the business section of Westcott Street. "What's that?"

She was pointing to Seven Rays, which is this great bookstore that specializes in what they call the mystic arts. The north side of the store, a solid brick wall about twenty feet high and eighty feet long, had been painted white from about six feet above the ground to the top. Sketchy black lines showed the outline of a forest, with mountains in the distance.

"Dave's getting his mural!" Norma shouted.

I knew Dave Davis was the owner of the store. But I didn't know anything about a mural.

"He's been wanting to have a mural painted on that wall for years," said Norma when I asked about it.

"How do you know that?" asked Chris. "I thought you only moved here two months ago."

"Honey, I work fast!" said Norma. Then she laughed that great laugh of hers.

I was happy. I thought the mural would fit well in our neighborhood, which is filled with great old houses and strange young people—well, strange people of all ages, actually.

About a mile from Westcott Street we started up a long hill. At the very top of the hill was an enormous, dark green house. It looked like the product of an architect's nightmare. Everything that could have been added to a house of that time had been added. The roof had three chimneys, two dormers, and a skylight. A long porch with big pillars stretched across the front. Some of the windows bowed out, some had diamond panes, and some were made of stained glass.

But the thing I liked best was the right corner—the east corner, I later figured out—which was a three-story tower. The roof of the tower was covered with black shingles; it tapered to a peak that made me think of a witch's hat.

The house was surrounded by more open land than most places in Syracuse. A winding stone sidewalk led up a broad lawn to the porch.

The lawn itself was bordered by the remains of a stone wall; the jagged chunks of broken rock looked like rotting teeth in some huge, prehistoric jaw.

Even though the place was rundown, I thought it was wonderful. As soon as Norma parked the truck, Chris and I jumped out.

As we did, I realized one more thing about Phoebe Watson's house.

It was haunted.

Very haunted.

CHAPTER THREE

The Painted Past

I turned to Chris. "Do you feel it?" I whispered.

Eyes wide, she nodded.

I could tell she was frightened. I was, too. The reason was simple: Until that moment, we had never known a place was haunted without somehow experiencing the ghost itself. Yet the instant we stepped out of Norma's truck, we knew there was a ghost somewhere nearby. It didn't show itself. It didn't touch us. We just knew it was there.

Waiting.

Waiting for Chris and me?

That didn't seem likely.

But if not for us, then who? And *why* did we know about it?

The last question was the only one I thought I might have an answer to. Chris and I have a theory that one reason we met Captain Gray was because our experience with the Woman in White had increased our sensitivity to spirits. Had our

16

second experience done the same thing? Had we started on some kind of spiral that would have us meet more ghosts, and become even more sensitive to the spirit world, so we would meet even *more* ghosts?

How long could that go on? Would our lives become crowded with ghosts that no one else could see? I hoped not. Much as I like being able to meet ghosts, I do want some kind of limit to it all!

Norma was halfway to the porch before she realized we weren't with her. She turned back to see what was keeping us. The look on our faces must have startled her because she asked, "What's wrong with you two? You look like you just saw . . ." Her voice trailed off. "Forget it. If you saw what you *look* like you saw, don't tell me. I promised Phoebe we would pick up this wardrobe, and I won't be able to do it if I'm all the time worried that someone is floating behind my shoulder."

I took a deep breath. "It's okay," I said, trying to reassure her. "Neither of us saw a ghost."

"Donteventalkaboutit!" cried Norma, so fast it all came out as one word. "Now, come on, before I change my mind. And if you see anything weird, *don't* tell me!"

We nodded and began to walk up the path.

I was frightened, but not terrified. After all, the ghosts we had met so far had actually been pretty nice.

The porch echoed hollowly under our feet.

Norma rang the doorbell. Phoebe took so long answering that I began to think that maybe *she* had died and the ghost we had sensed was hers. It wasn't until she opened the door and we started to follow her into the parlor that I remembered how slowly she moved.

The parlor was almost pretty. It had a high ceiling, dark blue wallpaper covered with little flowers, and an Oriental rug. The October light streamed in through three tall windows. Clearly the room had once been beautiful. But it looked slightly shabby now, and somehow empty, as if it should have had more furniture than it did. The only decorations were a painting that hung above the fireplace and a large Oriental vase.

The one thing in the room that *didn't* look worn out was the person sitting in the blue armchair. He was probably about sixty years old, but he had a full head of thick, silvery-white hair. He was dressed in business clothes and looked very formal except for his tie, which was bright red and covered with images of large, fan-tailed goldfish. He stood as we entered the room. Crossing toward us, he said, "You must be Norma Bliss! I'm so pleased to meet you!"

Norma looked surprised. "I didn't know I was so famous," she said with a slight laugh.

"Phoebe has told me all about you."

"This is Stephen Bassett, Norma," Phoebe said. "He's a very dear friend of mine. Now, why don't you introduce the girls, while I go get some tea things."

"Make mine coffee," said Norma.

As Phoebe left the room, Norma began to introduce us.

Mr. Bassett raised a hand to stop her. "No need for an introduction. I know who they are."

"You do?" I asked in surprise.

"You are Nina Tanleven, aren't you?"

Judging from the way he laughed, I must have appeared even more surprised than Norma had. "Don't be so worried. You live up the street from me. I know your father. And I assume you're Chris Gurley," he continued, turning to Chris.

"How do you know that?" asked Chris.

"You two did gain a certain notoriety after your adventure in the Grand Theater this past summer," Mr. Bassett said. "The newspapers covered the story, in case you forgot."

I was starting to like this guy. I figured I might learn something from him.

"You have the advantage on us, Stephen," said Norma. "Why not tell us what brings *you* here?"

"Business," he said, and shrugged.

Norma frowned. "Don't tell me you're an antique dealer, too. My business is tough enough as it is."

"I'm Phoebe's lawyer," he said. I could hear a hint of steel in his voice. "If you want to know any-

thing beyond that, you'll have to ask Phoebe herself."

I had a feeling tht Norma wanted to give him
a big "Well, excu-u-u-use me!" But she held it in
and said something polite, and pretty soon the two
of them were involved in a conversation that I
thought was totally boring.

It didn't seem like the kind of situation where
we were going to learn anything. So when Chris
made a gesture with her head, I was glad to follow
her over to look at the painting that hung above
the fireplace.

At first I thought it was just a pretty picture
of a forest. Then I realized there were dead bodies
scattered among the fallen leaves. After I spotted
the first few, I couldn't miss them. My eyes began
picking out more and more, almost as if I were
staring at one of those find-the-hidden-object pictures.

Some of the bodies were marked with terrible
wounds.

My head began to whirl. For a moment the
painting seemed to take me in. I could hear the
moans of dying men, the deep thud of cannons in
the distance. The air around me felt cold and wet.
It was filled with the smell of fire and blood.

I tried to look away. To my horror, I couldn't
move. The picture had trapped me and was forcing
me to see things I didn't want to know about.

CHAPTER FOUR

In the Tower

I started to panic. I wanted to turn from those terrible images. But I couldn't. I couldn't escape the blood and the death—until Phoebe came back into the room and asked, "Well, now, who wants what?"

Her voice broke the picture's terrible hold on me. Shivering, I spun away. I wanted to ask Chris if she had felt the same thing, but I would have to wait until we were alone. Then I saw her eyes, and I knew I didn't have to ask. She had felt it, too.

Before anyone could answer Phoebe's question, the doorbell rang.

"That must be Carla," said Phoebe. "Goodness, I can't remember the last time I had so many visitors." She turned to Stephen and said, "I didn't expect everything to happen at once like this. I'm sorry."

"Don't worry about it," Mr. Bassett said, waving his hand.

Phoebe hobbled off to answer the door. While she was gone, I pointed to the painting and asked softly, "What *is* that?"

"It's called 'Early Harvest'," said Mr. Bassett. He grimaced. "Dreadful, isn't it? Very famous, though."

Before I could ask why it was famous, Phoebe returned. Following her was a tall, white-haired woman dressed in a dark blue silk blouse and a pair of jeans that had faded to light blue. Her eyes were blue, too—ice blue in a face that was tanned and wrinkled. Although she looked only a few years younger than Phoebe, she seemed a lot stronger.

"Carla!" Norma cried. "What are you doing here?"

The tone in Norma's voice made it clear that she was really happy to see Carla. But the white-haired woman drew back a little, as if someone had made a rude noise.

Norma just laughed. "Sorry," she said. "I didn't mean to be nosy. I mean, I am nosy, but I try to keep it under control. I'm just surprised to see you!"

Carla relaxed a little. "Actually, I'm a little surprised to see you, too," she said. She spoke slowly, and her voice had a musical quality to it that I liked very much.

Norma gestured for Chris and me to join them. "Girls, this is Carla Bond. She teaches art history at the university. I use her as a consultant when I'm having trouble figuring out the date for a piece of furniture. She's the best in the city."

Carla Bond smiled at the praise. "Pleased to meet you," she said after Norma had told her our names. She was formal, but not stiff. She held out her hand, which felt cool and smooth in my own when we shook. She smelled like peaches.

Ms. Bond had just let go of my hand when a large black-and-white cat wandered into the room and began rubbing against Norma's legs. Norma jumped back with a little cry.

"General Pershing!" Phoebe exclaimed. "How did you get in here?" Moving stiffly, she bent to pick up the cat, which hissed angrily. "I'm sorry, Norma," said Phoebe. "I'll put him outside."

"I'm allergic," Norma explained to the rest of us as Phoebe shuffled away.

After a moment of slightly awkward silence, Ms. Bond turned to Norma and said, "I expect you'll find some excellent pieces here. Phoebe's family was quite prominent in Syracuse before the tragedy."

My ears perked up. "Tragedy?" I asked. "What tragedy?"

I must have sounded too eager, because Ms. Bond gave me an exaggerated version of the look she had given Norma. "The family fell on hard times," she said softly.

Then she turned and went to sit on the couch.

"Curiosity killed the cat," Chris whispered, with a smirk.

I know that's supposed to mean you can get into trouble by poking your nose in places where it doesn't belong—but at the moment I felt that curiosity was going to kill me all by itself. I wanted to know what had happened so badly, I thought I might pop.

It wasn't just what my dad calls *idle* curiosity either. Ghosts and tragedies seem to go together. Whatever the tragedy was, it probably explained why the place felt haunted.

Of course, Carla Bond's reaction had made me even more curious.

I glanced at the three adults sitting on the couch. Norma looked as curious as I felt. I could tell she was dying to know what Ms. Bond was doing here, but didn't dare ask.

Phoebe reappeared at the door with a tea cart. "Well, that's better," she said, rolling it into the room. "Now we can chat for a moment."

She poured tea for everyone except Norma, then passed around a plate of little cookies, and it was all very nice. But it didn't last very long because after about ten minutes Mr. Bassett glanced at his watch and said, "I hate to be unsociable, but I have to get going soon."

Norma took the hint. "Actually, we'd better get moving, too. No need to climb the stairs, Phoebe. I know where it is."

Phoebe looked at her gratefully.

When we were back out in the hall, Norma said, "I've got to get my toolbox. Why don't you two go on up. Turn right at the top of the stairs. You'll find the room at the end of the hall. I'll be there in a few minutes."

She turned and went out the door. Chris and I wandered up the stairway, which had wide steps covered by a dark red rug. The rug was faded, and almost worn through in spots, but you could tell it had once been very elegant.

The striped wallpaper was faded, too, and several places at the top and the bottom were starting to peel.

"Looks like she's been selling off the family portraits," said Chris, pointing to a series of rectangles where the wallpaper's colors were less faded. "Poor old lady must really be broke."

"Who would want pictures of someone else's relatives?" I asked.

"All right, so maybe it wasn't the relatives," Chris said. "Maybe Phoebe had paintings of clowns hanging here. Or purple and green daisies. The point is, something used to be here, and now it's gone."

The talk of paintings reminded me of something else. "What was that all about—that thing that happened when we were looking at the picture downstairs?"

"I don't know," Chris said, her eyes wide. "But it sure felt creepy."

I nodded. Actually, this whole place was slightly creepy. Sad, too, I realized.

That feeling of sadness didn't come from the house's slightly rundown look. I don't think it came from anything you could *see*. My father says old houses take on a personality from all the living that's gone on inside them. He's not usually superstitious, but he does restore old buildings for a living, so I figure he ought to know.

By the time we reached the top of the stairs, I decided Phoebe Watson's house had seen a *lot* of sadness. I wondered again about the tragedy Carla Bond had mentioned. Then I shook myself, trying to shrug away the feeling of sorrow.

We were standing in a long hallway. To our left was another stairway. We turned right, as Norma had told us, and headed for the end of the hall.

"Good," whispered Chris. "It's in the tower."

I smiled. I was dying to see the tower rooms myself.

"Oooh!" Chris exclaimed when we opened the door. "I want to live here!"

I felt the same way.

The room was about fifteen feet across, with a high ceiling, dark green wallpaper, and woodwork that had never seen a paintbrush. (Painting over the woodwork is this terrible thing that has happened to most of the old houses around here.)

The curve of the tower was created by short walls that met at broad angles, making the outline of the floor look like the edge of a stop sign. All but the three inner walls had large, diamond-paned windows made of thick glass, beveled on the edges to create extra reflections and rainbows.

Except for two pieces of furniture, the room was empty.

One piece of furniture was the big brass bed that sat in the center of the room. It had four shiny posts topped with large knobs. Curved brass pipes at the head and foot of the bed made fanciful swirls between the posts. An old-fashioned patchwork quilt covered the mattress.

"That's the kind of bed I always wanted," I said.

"It's gorgeous," agreed Chris. "But I like this better. It makes me think of Narnia."

She was pointing to the other piece of furniture in the room, the large wardrobe that stood against one wall.

"Big, isn't it?" I said.

"And beautiful," said Chris.

We walked over to look at it. The wardrobe was about eight feet tall and four feet wide—so big it was like a whole closet standing separate from the wall. I wondered how we were going to get it into the truck.

Most of it was made of reddish-brown wood. Carved panels ran across the top and bottom. On them were thick, scrolling designs that looked like knotted ropes made of wood. On the door was a huge mirror. The glass was dark, and streaked with age.

I looked at our reflections as we walked toward the wardrobe. Chris was a couple of inches taller than me. Her reddish-blond hair was a lot more interesting than mine, I thought. My hair was a plain dark brown.

We stood side by side for a moment, staring at ourselves. Suddenly I caught my breath. In the dark glass of the mirror, I saw a ghost take shape in the bed behind us.

CHAPTER FIVE

Watched, by Unseen Eyes

Not saying a word, barely moving, I tipped my head in the direction of the bed and mouthed, "Do you see?"

Chris, looking not at me but at my reflection, nodded.

The ghost was a little girl, probably not more than six years old. She wore an old-fashioned nightgown and clutched a rag doll. The look on her face was so sad it almost made me cry.

"Let's turn around," mouthed Chris's reflection.

It was my turn to nod. Slowly, silently, we turned back to face the bed. But as we did, Norma came bounding into the room with her toolbox.

"Look at that bed!" she shrieked.

At once the ghost faded out of sight.

"Did you see it?" I asked in astonishment.

"Of course I've seen it before," said Norma, misunderstanding my question. "I've been trying to get Phoebe to sell it to me for over a year now. It would be perfect for the shop."

"Should we tell her?" I whispered as Norma turned back to admire the bed.

Chris shrugged. "She said she didn't want to hear anything about ghosts. I guess if she didn't notice it was there, it won't hurt her."

Norma stood at the foot of the bed, holding on to the brass tubes. "Actually, I've offered Phoebe more than this is worth," she said, "just because it would look so good in the shop. But she absolutely refuses to sell. Sentimental attachment, I guess."

I wondered if Phoebe's "attachment" was because she knew her bed was haunted.

I stared at the bed, trying to sense the ghost. It was frustrating because I didn't really know what to do. If I was trying to see better, I would squint. If I was trying to smell something, I might sniff. But since I don't know *how* I sense ghosts, I didn't know how to try harder.

Where had the little girl gone? Where *do* ghosts go when you can't see them? Are they still there, just invisible? Do they float off to some ghost place?

I wish I knew.

I glanced at Chris. She shook her head, signaling that she could no longer detect the ghost either.

I was so wound up about the ghost, I forgot the real reason we were there until Norma's voice brought me back to reality. "Actually, this is almost as good as the bed," she said, admiring the wardrobe. "Won't take much work to get it in shape either. Well, the first thing we have to do is move it away from the wall. Time to flex your muscles, ladies."

Working together, the three of us were able to slide the wardrobe across the floor without much trouble. We found two things behind it: a pile of dust bunnies and a little door. The door was definitely more interesting than the dust. About two feet high and two feet wide, it was located nearly halfway up the wall. Next to it was a brass square with a pair of buttons inside.

"Well, look at that," said Norma. "An old dumbwaiter!"

"What's a dumbwaiter?" asked Chris.

"Sounds like the guy who took my order at McDonald's yesterday," I replied.

Norma sighed. "A dumbwaiter is like a little elevator for food. Here, I'll show you." She opened the door. Behind it was a box. "They used to load this in the kitchen," said Norma. "Then the meal could be delivered straight to the room without anyone having to climb the stairs. Dirty dishes got sent down the same way."

"Neat!" I said. "I want one."

"I'd settle for my own refrigerator," said Chris.

"How about we settle for taking that wardrobe apart?" Norma asked.

The job was simpler than I expected, mostly because Norma really knows about that kind of thing. After we had been working for a few minutes, I had a feeling that someone was watching us. I looked around. I couldn't see anyone.

But the sensation wouldn't go away.

"Do you feel it?" I whispered to Chris while Norma was concentrating on a large, boltlike contraption.

She nodded. "She's back, but she's not letting us see her."

I wondered if we should warn Norma that we were being watched by a spirit. At first I couldn't see any point in scaring her away from a piece of furniture that would probably make a good profit for her. After a while, though, I started feeling guilty—as if I had been caught taking something that didn't belong to me. But what could I do? Even if we talked Norma out of buying the wardrobe, Phoebe would just sell it to someone else. And I was pretty sure she wouldn't sell it at all if she didn't really need the money.

Since opening my mouth would only cause trouble without creating a solution, I didn't say anything. But when I caught Chris's eye, I could tell she was getting the same kinds of vibrations I was.

Norma interrupted my thoughts by yelling, "You come out of there right this instant!"

I jumped. For a second I thought she was talking to the ghost. Then I realized she was shouting at the bolt. It seemed to work, too. At least, the thing started to turn.

"That's right!" Norma said happily. "That's right! Oh, honey, when I talk, these babies *know* they better listen!"

Once Norma had the top loose, we realized none of us were tall enough to lift it off the wardrobe. We needed something to stand on. So Norma sent Chris and me downstairs to borrow a couple of chairs.

I was a little worried about leaving Norma alone in the room. But the ghost didn't seem as if it was going to cause any trouble. So down we went.

When we stepped into the parlor, Phoebe was dabbing at her eyes, the way she had done when I first met her. Carla Bond and Mr. Bassett looked uncomfortable.

"Norma wants to borrow a couple of chairs," announced Chris.

Everybody seemed to find this confusing. But once we explained why, Phoebe told us we would find some sturdy wooden chairs in the kitchen. "It's at the end of the hall," she added.

"Well, I say it's blackmail," Chris said, as we stepped into the kitchen.

"What?"

"Blackmail. Ms. Bond and Mr. Bassett have got something on Phoebe, and they're taking her for all she's worth. That's why she's selling off the furniture—so she can pay them to keep quiet."

I laughed. "That is the dumbest theory you've come up with yet. What secrets could a sweet little old lady like Phoebe have?"

"Maybe she's a drug dealer."

"You watch too much TV," I said.

"Well, you can't trust anyone these days."

I picked up a chair. "Let's get these upstairs before Norma realizes she's not alone."

We started back toward the stairway. But halfway along the hall we heard a horrible racket in the parlor. Then someone began to scream.

We dropped the chairs.

"Come on!" Chris shouted. Grabbing me by the arm, she rushed toward the parlor. Bursting through the door, we found Phoebe, Ms. Bond and Mr. Bassett standing in a half circle, staring at the windows.

The noise was louder in here, almost unbearable.

It took me a moment to figure out what was causing it.

Once I did, I felt a chill crawl down my spine.

CHAPTER SIX

Panic in the Parlor

The shutters that covered the center window were flapping back and forth, as if outside a pair of giant hands kept yanking them open and slamming them shut.

For a moment I thought it must be the wind. But the shutters on the other windows weren't moving at all. Through those windows you could see that the evening was clear and still; not a hint of a breeze stirred the leaves of the big oak outside. Yet the shutters on the center window continued their wild slamming until Phoebe suddenly pressed her hands against her ears and screamed, "Stop!"

Immediately the banging stopped. For a moment everything was silent.

Phoebe was the first to speak. "He doesn't want me to do it," she moaned. "He doesn't want me to do it!"

"Skip the act, Phoebe!" snapped Carla Bond. "If you didn't want to go through with the deal, you didn't have to set up this show. A simple no would have been sufficient."

I expected Mr. Bassett to defend Phoebe. But before he could speak, Norma came running into the room.

"What's going on down here?" she demanded. Without waiting for anyone to answer, she took in the scene, the looks on everyone's faces, and said, "Forget I asked that. I don't think I want to know."

"It's all right, Norma," Phoebe said softly. "You're not doing anything wrong."

This sentence seemed to worry Norma enormously. "I changed my mind again," she said. "Tell me what's going on."

"We were working on a contract," Mr. Bassett explained, his brown eyes wide, his voice husky. "Phoebe was about to sign it. But when she picked up the pen, the shutters began to slam back and forth." He swallowed, his eyes opening even wider as he remembered the scene. "They just began to slam," he repeated. "Back and forth, back and . . ."

His voice trailed off.

"I knew I shouldn't do this." Phoebe moaned.

"Do what?" Norma asked.

"It's a private deal," said Carla Bond, who seemed calmer now. "And nobody is forcing her. I'm disappointed in you, Phoebe. I'm going to go now. If you change your mind and want to do this without the dramatics, let me know."

Looking very upset, she turned and left the room. The odor of peaches lingered behind her.

"Does she really think I set this up?" asked Phoebe, still staring at the window.

"I don't know what she thinks," said Mr. Bassett. "I don't know what *I* think, Phoebe. It's not that I don't trust you. But this kind of thing just doesn't happen. It's probably easier for someone like Carla to think you set it up than to believe—well, to believe whatever just happened here." He sank into his chair. "Look at *me!*"

He lifted his hands, which were trembling violently. "What am *I* supposed to believe? That there's a ghost opposed to our deal?"

"I know what I believe," Norma said. "I believe it's time we got out of here!"

"Don't go!" cried Phoebe. "Please, Norma. It's not the wardrobe. You can take that. Really. It's fine, as long as you don't take the bed."

Norma's eyes got even wider, which I wouldn't have thought was possible. "What do you mean, 'Don't take the bed'?"

Phoebe shook her head. "Just don't take the bed," she whispered.

"Well, I wasn't going to," Norma said. "You wouldn't sell it to me, in case you forgot."

Chris nudged me in the ribs. "Can you sense a ghost here?" she whispered.

I shook my head.

"Me neither. Whatever was banging those shutters is gone—at least for now."

"Maybe it was never here," I replied.

Chris looked puzzled.

"Maybe it was outside all along," I said softly.

She nodded her agreement.

". . . better sit down," Mr. Bassett was saying. "You look awfully pale."

Phoebe nodded vaguely. "I guess you're right," she said. She sank into her chair, then dropped her head into her hands. "Oh, what am I going to do?"

"Don't worry," Mr. Bassett said. "If you really want to—"

He stopped and looked in our direction. "Norma, I need some time to speak with my client. Would you mind?"

"I don't mind." Norma paused, then looked right at Mr. Bassett and added fiercely, "Not so long as you treat her right."

Phoebe gave us a thin smile. "Don't worry, Norma. Stephen takes good care of me. I don't know what I'd do without him." She reached out and patted the lawyer's hand. "Now, you ladies had best go get that wardrobe."

Norma nodded, and Chris and I followed her out of the room. "Do you suppose it would be too wicked to stand out here and listen?" she whispered once we had closed the parlor door behind us.

I had been wondering the same thing myself. After all, if Phoebe was in trouble, we had to know what it was before we could help her. But Norma quickly thought better of that idea. "Fine example I am," she muttered. "Your father would have my hide if he knew I was teaching you to be an eavesdropper."

"Actually, my father can be *very* nosy," I said encouragingly.

For a second Norma seemed to be wavering. But then she said firmly, "Come on. Pick up those chairs, and let's go do our job."

She made it up three steps before she turned around and said, "What am I doing? Let's leave!"

"What about the wardrobe?" asked Chris. She set the chair down.

"Forget the wardrobe!"

"Phoebe really wants us to take it," I said, setting my chair down as well.

Norma took a deep breath. She looked from Chris to me, then back again. "All right. You two are the experts. Tell it to me straight. Is it safe up there?"

"As far as we can tell," I said.

"Safe enough that *we* don't mind going up," Chris added. "We'll even go first if you want."

Norma shook her head. "I'm the leader of this expedition," she muttered. Taking another deep breath, she started up the stairs again.

Even though we had decided not to eavesdrop, Norma's hesitation had left me in the hall long enough to hear Mr. Bassett say, "Phoebe, if you would just sell that picture, you could keep the house."

I picked up the chair again, then followed Norma and Chris up the stairs, thinking about what I had heard. Why couldn't Phoebe keep her house? Because she was broke, probably. But why would selling a picture take care of the problem? Could she really have a picture worth that much? And what picture was the lawyer talking about? The one over the fireplace?

I shivered at the memory of the grisly images and wondered why anyone would paint such a thing to begin with. Could a painting like that possibly be worth enough to let Phoebe stay in her house? If it was, then why didn't she sell it? I would have been glad to trade something like that for my house. Heck, I'd have *given* it away, rather than have to look at it every day.

I was so wrapped up in my thoughts that I forgot what we were there for until Norma said, "Well, child, are you going to put down that chair or not?"

"Don't mind her, Norma," said Chris, who was already standing on the chair she had carried up. "She gets that way when she's thinking."

I made a face at her and set the chair on the floor. Norma climbed up. Working together, she and Chris lifted the top off the wardrobe.

Even in pieces the wardrobe was heavy, and it took all three of us to carry some of the sections down the stairs. After we had most of it on the porch, Norma went to open the back of the truck. Chris and I went upstairs to get the top, which was the last and smallest piece.

As we were carrying the top out of the room, I heard someone start to cry. I turned back to look and almost lost my grip on the wood when I saw a little girl sitting in the bed.

"Chris!" I hissed. "Do you see?"

"I see," she whispered.

The little girl continued her quiet weeping. I wanted to comfort her. But what could I do? Put my arms around her? Pat her on the shoulder? If I tried to touch her, my hand would go right through her.

Before I could decide what to do, the form in the bed faded away. But her voice lingered in the air after her image was gone, the way the smell of peaches had remained in the room after Carla Bond left.

"Daddy?" she whispered softly and sadly. "Oh, Daddy, when are you coming back?"

CHAPTER SEVEN

The Lost Masterpiece

"What are we going to do?" Chris asked, looking up at me. I was sitting on a branch of the apple tree in her backyard. Before I could answer, she swung one leg over the branch and pulled herself up to sit beside me.

"I'm not sure," I said, moving over to make room for her.

We were sitting in Chris's apple tree instead of her house because finding a quiet spot to talk *in* the Gurley house is about as likely as finding a giraffe in your bathtub. That's because Chris has more brothers than a bug has legs. I keep trying to count them—her brothers, not a bug's legs—but they're never all around at the same time. Whenever I ask Chris how many there are, she just shrugs and says, "About five more than I need." (But she won't tell me how many she thinks she needs.)

Anyway, if you want to talk quietly, it's easier to go outside—especially on a night when the air is cool and crisp and filled with the smells of October. I felt good. I was upset by what had happened that day, but I was also excited about the fact that we had landed in the middle of a new mystery. I love mysteries. Solving them makes me feel really alive.

"Well, we've got to do something," Chris said.

"I agree. It gives me the creeps to think of that poor little girl, waiting there for her father."

"She's probably been waiting for years," said Chris sourly. "Another few weeks won't kill her."

"That's not funny!" I slid along the branch and reached for an apple.

"So it was a bad joke. But I mean it about waiting. Much as I'd like to help that little kid, Phoebe's the one I'm really worried about."

The apple was wormy. I threw it on the ground.

"You're right," I said. "I hate the thought of her losing her home. Of course, if she wasn't so stubborn about that hideous picture, she wouldn't have to."

"That's assuming you believe what Mr. Bassett said," replied Chris. "My father says you shouldn't believe anything you hear from a lawyer."

"I thought your uncle was a lawyer."

Chris laughed. "He's the reason my dad says that!"

That night I dreamed I was sleeping in a bed where someone had died. I woke with a shout. It took me a long time to get back to sleep.

Chris's mother had some errands to do on our side of town the next afternoon, so she drove me home. I almost fell over when I walked through our front door. The stairway looked like a disaster area.

Actually, our stairway has always looked like a disaster area—mostly because it's covered with a truly hideous wallpaper. At least, it used to be. At the moment that wallpaper, which had been there for as long as I could remember, was half gone. It lay in soggy piles on the steps. It hung in long, wet strips from the wall. Scraps of it still clung here and there. In the middle of all this stood my father, belting out "The Stripper" and shaking his hips as he ran a blade up the wall.

"Dad! What's going on?"

"The cobbler's children are getting new shoes!" he replied happily.

I thought about that remark for several seconds before I decided there was no way I was going to make any sense out of it. "What are you talking about?" I asked.

"It's an old saying: 'The shoemaker's children go barefoot.'"

"Kind of a dumb saying, isn't it?"

"Not really. It means the guy who makes shoes is usually so busy making them for everyone else, he never gets around to making them for his own kids. Therefore, the shoemaker's children go barefoot. This weekend I realized you were a shoemaker's child."

"My feet are fine," I said, pointing to my sneakers. "Though I would like a nice pair of leather boots, and—"

"Wrong idea!" said Dad. He pointed the scraper blade at me and asked, "What do I do for a living?"

Before I could point out that the answer to *that* question had been up in the air since he quit his job to go freelance, he answered it himself.

"I restore old buildings. But have I ever restored *this* place? It is to laugh! I have been too busy. I finally decided it was time to do something about this joint."

"But *you* don't do this kind of stuff," I said, stepping over a pile of soggy wallpaper. "You plan it, then have other people do the work."

"So this will be good for me," he said, running his scraper under a strip of wallpaper. "I get to see what I ask other people to do. Come on—give me a hand."

He gave me a blade and showed me how to peel off the paper without damaging the wall underneath. The paper came off fairly easily because he had already soaked it with a stripper solution. Peeling it was kind of fun—a little like picking at a giant scab.

"I had forgotten how ugly this stuff really is," I said, as I pulled away a large section of gray and purple stripes.

My father shrugged. "If you live with something long enough, it's easy to stop looking at it."

"So what made you see this again?"

"I have to confess—Norma inspired me. Have you been inside her house?"

"No. Have you?" *And what were you doing there if you were?* I wanted to add. But I bit my tongue.

"I had coffee with her the other day. I was amazed. She's only lived there two months, and she's already stripped the woodwork and re-papered the walls. All of them. I know people who take years to get that much done."

"This isn't going to be like the garden, is it?" I asked, looking at the half-stripped stairwell.

"Nine, you wound me!"

"Truth hurts," I said, as I ran my blade under a stray patch of paper. Dad had started a garden in the backyard three years ago—and I do mean *started*. Digging it up is as far as he got. The patch still sits there—dug up, and nothing more.

In a way I hope he never finishes it. It's very useful to me as it is, since I can mention it whenever he gets on my case about my not finishing things that *I* start.

On the other hand, he started the garden just before my mother left. So maybe I shouldn't be too rough on him about it. He didn't concentrate too well for a while back then.

Still, I really didn't want to live with the hall looking like *this* for the next three years.

Dad started to say something to defend himself, slipped on a piece of wet paper, and announced that it was time for a break. "I think we've got some slopnuggets around," he said.

Slopnuggets are these cookies the two of us make. They always come out different because we don't have a recipe. When we want to make some, we just take a big mixing bowl and throw in everything that seems as if it might make a good cookie that night. As long as we make sure to use the basic stuff like eggs and flour, and go light on things like pickles and pepper, they come out just fine. They're a little *weird* sometimes, but we've never made a batch we couldn't eat.

"So how was your weekend?" Dad asked as he set the milk and cookies on the dining room table.

"Interesting." I scooped a giant pile of orange fur off a chair and sat down. The fur blob was really our cat, Sidney. He batted halfheartedly at my leg and then stalked away, his belly swaying from side to side.

"I think he's getting fatter," I said.

"He's just putting on his winter pork," said my father, dunking a slopnugget into his coffee. "I shudder to ask this, but why was your weekend so interesting?"

I stared out the window into our backyard, where our single tree, an enormous maple, was beginning to litter the ground with red and orange leaves. "Did you ever hear of a painting called 'Early Harvest'?" I asked at last.

"Sure. One of the most famous war pictures ever painted. Quite well known locally, of course."

"How come?"

He got that superior look grown-ups get when they're about to tell you something they think you're incredibly stupid not to have known in the first place. I already knew his next line ("What *do* they teach you in those schools these days?"), so I waited until he got that out of his system before I really started to listen.

"'Early Harvest' was painted by Syracuse's own mad genius." He sounded wistful, as if he thought it was wonderful to be a crazy artist. "His name was Cornelius Fletcher. He grew up right here, painted a handful of the best pictures ever created by an American, and then stopped."

"I suppose nobody realized how great he was until he died."

Dad shook his head. "Surprisingly, he gained a fair amount of acclaim while he was still living. That's one reason it was such a puzzle when he stopped painting. Of course, the fact that he stopped when he did is one reason his pictures are so valuable—there just aren't enough of them to go around. Most American museums would love to get their hands on an original Cornelius Fletcher. Although what they really want are the postwar canvases. His work was pretty bland until after the war."

"Which war?"

"World War One—the war to end all wars."

"If that was the war to end all wars, how come we had World War Two?"

Dad shrugged. "It didn't work," he said sadly.

I decided to change the subject. "How much are we talking about when we say 'valuable'?"

He rolled his eyes back, as if he were consulting some calculator in his brain. "Probably a hundred thousand," he said. "Maybe more."

"Dollars?"

"No, goldfish! Of course dollars. But that's nothing compared to what the Lost Masterpiece would fetch."

This time I really paid attention. "Lost Masterpiece?"

"Only a rumor. Gossip has it that Fletcher was working on his greatest picture when he finally went around the bend. No one knows what happened to it. One of the great mysteries of American art."

"What would that be worth?" I asked.

"A few million, I suppose. Dollars, not goldfish. But don't get excited. I doubt that it really exists."

Typical grown-up negative thinking.

"How come he went mad?"

"I don't know. It's been a while since I read up on this. I think it was some kind of family tragedy. Actually, I don't believe anyone really knows the details. Why are you so interested in all this?"

"I saw the picture yesterday," I said.

"In a book?"

"No, on someone's wall."

"Strange, isn't it," he said. "You wouldn't think anyone would want that print hanging in their house. But it was quite popular for a while among people who were opposed to wars. You'll see a framed copy in antique shops every now and then."

"I don't think this was a print," I said, filling him in on what had happened when Chris and I had been looking at the picture.

My father's eyes widened. "At it again, are we?" he said at last.

I shrugged. "We saw a ghost, too."

"What kind of ghost?"

"A little kid. She was crying for her daddy."

My father closed his eyes; he looked as though he were in pain.

"Are you all right?"

He nodded. "Just a little sad."

"How come?"

"Well, think about it. Ghosts tend to hang around when they have some unfinished business—usually around the place they died. From what you heard, I would guess your insubstantial friend died while waiting for her father. Maybe you wouldn't understand, but I can't think of anything worse than not—well, not coming through for you if you needed me."

I stood up and walked around the table. "You've been coming through for me, Dad," I said softly.

He patted my hand. "Come on. Let's go strip wallpaper."

I followed him into the hall, wondering what tragedy had left a little girl's ghost waiting in Phoebe Watson's house.

CHAPTER EIGHT

Past Imperfect

When I called Chris to tell her what I had found out from my father, she said, "A crazy painter, huh? I suppose you could say he had a 'brush with madness.'"

I refused to satisfy her with a groan. "What are we going to do about all this?" I asked, trying to get the conversation back on track.

"We start by getting more information."

"Any suggestions?"

"Sure. We go to the library. If this Fletcher guy was so hot, we ought to be able to learn *something* about him there. Of course, we don't know that the picture has anything to do with anything else, but it's as good a place to start as any."

"Do you suppose Sam still works in the reference room?"

Sam was a librarian we got to know while we were trying to solve the mystery at the Grand Theater. He had the most gorgeous eyes of any librarian I had ever met. In fact, he was pretty gorgeous in general.

"We're going there to learn about the dead," said Chris, "not to long for the living."

"Life goes on," I replied, trying to sound casual.

Actually, by the time I met Chris at the library Monday afternoon, I wasn't so sure life *was* going to go on. I had been so wound up in the weekend's events that I never got around to doing my homework. My teacher was not amused; somehow, I didn't think my father would be either.

"You'd better get your act together, or your dad's going to nail your feet to the floor," was the way Chris put it.

I had a feeling she was right.

"Hey!" Sam said, when we walked into the reference room. "It's my ghost-bustin' buddies. What's up, ladies?"

I raised my left eyebrow, a trick I had spent about six months trying to perfect. "More mystery," I whispered.

Sam looked from side to side, as if he were afraid someone in the room might be a spy. Lowering his voice, he whispered back, "What is it this time?"

"Ve vant to know about zis arteest named Corneeelius Fletcher," Chris said, slipping into her secret agent accent.

"Zen you should go to ze art and music section!"

"I get confused," I said, dropping the game. "I never know where I'm supposed to start in this place."

"Start by asking a librarian," said Sam. "That's why we're here."

The woman in Art and Music had jet black hair and skin the color most beach freaks spend all summer trying to get. Only you could tell *her* skin was just naturally that color. According to the sign on her desk, her name was Olivia de la Pena. She was sticking labels on some compact discs when we walked up. When she saw us, she stopped what she was doing and asked if she could help us.

We told her what we wanted.

"No one has written a biography of Cornelius Fletcher yet." She sighed. "Lord knows I could use one—I've got high school students in here all the time trying to learn about him for papers on local history. But I do have one thing that might help."

She stood up and led us to a book called *Twentieth-Century American Artists*. It had a half page of small print on Cornelius Fletcher, along with a black-and-white copy of "Early Harvest." Next to the photo, in tiny letters, were the words "Courtesy of Phoebe Watson."

"That settles that," said Chris, pointing to the credit line. "The picture's the real thing."

"It's still hideous," I said.

"I tend to agree with you," said Ms. de la Pena. "On the other hand, it *is* considered one of the most powerful antiwar paintings ever done. That was a real change for Fletcher, of course. He was just a landscape painter until after he came back from France. But that's all in here," she said. "I'll let you find out for yourselves."

She went back to her compact discs. Unfortunately, there wasn't that much more to find out. According to the book, Cornelius Fletcher was born in Syracuse in 1890, got married in 1915, went off to war in 1917, and died in 1924. The book did mention the Lost Masterpiece, but only as an example of art world gossip.

"Find what you were looking for?" asked Ms. de la Pena, when she saw us close the book.

I shrugged. "I would have liked a few more details," I said. "Like how he died."

"I don't know how he died," said Ms. de la Pena. "But I can tell you how he lost his legs."

"Lost his legs?" Chris asked.

"It's a fairly nasty story," said Ms. de la Pena. She frowned. "Actually, I'm not the best one to tell it. Since you're so interested, you might want to wait a little while. I think Marcus is going to be in today."

"Who's Marcus?" I asked.

"A student at the university. He's doing his thesis on Fletcher, and he comes here to use the local history section. Does a lot of digging in the newspapers from Fletcher's period. Spends time in the genealogy section, too. All that obscure stuff graduate students feed on. He's been working on it for nearly a year now. I wish he'd finish. If it's good enough, maybe he'll get it published and make my job easier."

We decided to wait. Except we're not very good at waiting, and after a few minutes Ms. de la Pena got sort of sick of us and suggested we take a trip to the reference room to look at some microfilms of newspapers from Fletcher's day.

"The last time we tried to look at microfilms, they had already been stolen," Chris said, referring to what had happened when we tried to do research on the Woman in White.

When Ms. de la Pena realized we were the ones who had *recovered* the stolen films, she acted as if we were celebrities. "Why didn't you tell me who you were? I'm so pleased to meet the two of you. I was *very* impressed with what you did this summer."

She went to the reference room with us and helped us pick out some microfilms that might be of use. We each took three or four of the fat spools over to the reading machines. Sitting side by side, we threaded them in and started to scan through them.

Let me tell you, you can learn a lot of weird stuff by looking at old papers.

For one thing, you learn that things today probably aren't as awful as people like to think. I found a bunch of stories about the kinds of grisly crimes that make people shake their heads and mutter, "What *is* this world coming to?" After looking at those papers, I'd say whatever we're coming to isn't that much different from what we were coming to seventy years ago.

On the other hand, movies were silent back then, liquor was illegal, chicken cost more than steak, and a car cost less than a good bicycle costs today. Of course, people got paid a lot less, too.

I didn't find anything about Cornelius Fletcher, but I didn't really mind. I was enjoying looking at the old papers. At least I was getting a better sense of the time he lived in.

I was reading an article about a fourteen-year-old girl who was suing her husband for divorce when a voice above us said, "You can spend months looking for information that way."

Chris and I turned around. Then we looked up because the man standing behind us was incredibly tall. He was also so skinny that I kind of worried he might break in half while he was standing there. He had rumpled black hair, big glasses, a huge nose and a friendly smile. The knees on his jeans were patched, a fact I noticed because they were so close to my eye level.

"You *are* Chris and Nine, aren't you?"

"I'm Nine. She's Chris."

"I understand you're interested in Cornelius Fletcher."

"Ms. de la Pena told us you knew how he lost his legs," Chris said.

Marcus nodded. "It's a pretty nasty story. Doesn't put this community in a very good light. Why do you want to know it?"

"We saw one of his paintings the other day, and it got us interested in him," I said.

Marcus looked more interested. "Which painting?"

I made a face. "'Early Harvest.'"

"You mean a print?"

"No, we saw the original," Chris said.

Suddenly Marcus looked very interested. "Then you've met the owner?"

"If you mean Phoebe Watson, then the answer is yes."

"All right, here's the deal; I'll tell you what I know, if you'll tell me what she's like."

Chris and I looked at each other.

"I've been trying to get an interview with her for over two years," said Marcus. He sounded a little desperate. "I need *something* about her for my thesis."

"Well, okay," I said, feeling confused.

Marcus seemed to relax a little. "Let's go over there," he said, gesturing to one of the library tables. "I'll tell you as much as I know of the story."

When we were all settled around the table, Marcus took off his glasses, rubbed them on his shirt, settled them back on his beaky nose, and began.

"Okay, here's what I've been able to figure out. It seems that when Cornelius Fletcher came back from the war, he was filled with despair over what he had seen. It was a terrible war, you know. I mean, they all are, but this one was something new in the history of the world—new kinds of weapons, new ways of fighting. Fletcher went over with stars in his eyes and came back with rage in his heart, particularly at the old men who ran the war and sent young men off to die."

I thought about "Early Harvest" and all the young men dying in the forest.

"His style of painting changed," Marcus continued, "became very political. It was a bad time for him to do that—at least, in terms of his own career. The country was going through a reactionary backlash, and freedom of speech had just about been thrown out the window. Poor Fletcher might have been all right if he had been living in Greenwich Village or someplace like that. But not around here. The more famous his work became, the more upset the reactionaries got. Finally a gang of them jumped him one night and 'taught him a lesson'—which is to say they beat him so badly that he nearly died."

"That's terrible!" I cried.

Marcus nodded. "What made it even worse was that he was already half crippled. His legs had been injured in the war, and he had to walk on crutches."

"They beat up a guy on crutches?" Chris asked in astonishment.

"They didn't like what he was painting," Marcus said. His voice was sharp with anger. "They left him in a ditch, and he had to crawl home. Only he couldn't get in, because the whole place was surrounded by a stone wall. Fletcher had locked the gate when he left, and now he couldn't reach it to unlock it. By the time somebody found him, his legs were so badly frostbitten, they had to be amputated. People mark that as the time when he began to move deeply into his insanity."

"What happened to the men who beat him up?" I asked.

"Most of them were never identified. The police weren't big on tracking down people who attacked suspected radicals; they figured Fletcher had it coming to him. You have to understand the times. During the war Congress actually passed a law that made it an offense to criticize the uniforms of the army."

"You mean you could be sent to jail for saying there was something wrong with the way soldiers dressed?" asked Chris.

"You got it," said Marcus.

I couldn't believe what I was hearing.

"Anyway," he continued, "it wasn't an atmosphere where the authorities had a lot of respect for people who spoke out against the official line. Even so, at least one of the men came to justice—the ringleader of the group, in fact."

"What happened to him?" asked Chris eagerly.

"His name was Hiram Potter. After the beating it came out that Fletcher had saved Potter's son's life during the war. The day Fletcher's legs were amputated, Potter went out to his barn and hung himself."

CHAPTER NINE

Art Lesson

I shivered. There's a lot about the past they don't teach you in school.

"What happened next?" Chris asked.

Marcus shrugged. "I've spent the better part of the last year trying to find that out. Unfortunately, it's still pretty much a mystery to me."

"Well, if we find anything, we'll let you know," Chris said.

Marcus laughed. I could feel myself begin to blush. Clearly he thought the idea that *we* might turn up something he hadn't already found himself was pretty ridiculous. Yet it wasn't a mean laugh. If anything, it was a little bitter. I had a feeling he was getting frustrated with his research.

"Just tell me what you know about Phoebe Watson," he said. "That will do for now."

We told him a shortened version of our visit to Phoebe's house—more about what Phoebe was like and how the painting was displayed than about what had happened there.

"Why is Phoebe so important to you anyway?" Chris asked when we were done. "I thought your paper was about Cornelius Fletcher."

Marcus gave us a knowing smile. "I guess you still have a few things to learn yourself," he said. "Phoebe Watson is Cornelius Fletcher's daughter."

He could see by our faces that he had scored with that piece of information. He let it sink in for a while, then told us that if we went over to the Everson Museum, we could see some more of Fletcher's work.

I wasn't all that eager to see more paintings like "Early Harvest." On the other hand, I couldn't think of anything else we should do next. So we left the library and headed for the museum, which was about three blocks away.

The quickest way to the museum was through Columbus Circle, which is this little plaza with a big statue of Christopher Columbus. It also has a nice fountain, a lot of pigeons, and a mix of business people and bums.

"That Marcus was a nice guy," said Chris as we crossed the circle.

"He seemed to be," I said. I was still a little boggled by what he had told us about Phoebe— and a little worried by what we had told him. "You don't suppose he's up to anything, do you?" I asked at last.

"Like what?"

"I don't know—trying to find the Lost Master-piece or something? Why else would he spend two years trying to get an interview with Phoebe?"

"College students are like that," Chris said. "Especially graduate students. One of my aunts spent three years studying fish intestines."

"Eeuw!"

I was still feeling disgusted when we got to the museum.

"Hey, this place is fabulous!" exclaimed Chris as we walked up to the building. I happened to agree with her. The Everson Museum looks like four big concrete boxes stuck together. The art-work starts before you even get inside; there are lots of big sculptures in a courtyard outside the building, including some you can walk through, and even a few you can climb on.

My favorites aren't for climbing, though. My favorites are these five clay towers, each about ten feet tall, that look as if they were made by some giant kindergarten kid who was losing his mind. I always get upset when I see them, though, because the green one has repair lines where they had to fix it after some jerk knocked the top off.

Chris spotted the towers as we were heading for the door. "Wait!" she cried. "I want to look at these!"

"Haven't you ever been here?" I asked, after she had examined them for a while.

She shook her head. "My parents aren't big on this kind of thing."

"Yeah, but I thought every kid in Syracuse got dragged through here on a field trip by the time they hit sixth grade."

"Maybe I was absent!" snapped Chris.

I decided to drop the matter.

We went inside.

When you enter the Everson, you find yourself in a huge space with an extra-high ceiling. A wide concrete staircase that looks as if there's nothing holding it up curls to the second floor.

We asked a guard where to find the Cornelius Fletcher paintings, and she sent us off in the right direction. "If you're lucky, you might even see Dr. Bond there," she said.

When we entered the room where Fletcher's pictures were hanging, I caught the smell of peaches. It wasn't until that moment that I connected the name Bond to the woman we had met at Phoebe's house on Saturday. I think it was the "Dr." part that threw me off.

Carla Bond seemed as surprised to see us as we were to see her. "Well, what brings you two here?"

I wanted to throw the question right back at her. Unfortunately, I knew that wouldn't do me much good. Adults can demand to know why kids are in a certain place, but kids don't have the same privilege when it comes to adults.

"We got interested in that painting we saw at Phoebe Watson's house and decided to find out more about it," Chris said. "Next thing we knew— here we were!"

I smiled. Chris had managed to answer Ms. Bond's question *and* let her know what she thought of the way she had asked it, all without crossing that invisible line labeled "smart aleck." She had stepped *close,* but she hadn't crossed it.

Ms. Bond's face twitched a little. "You must be very interested in art to go to all this trouble."

"Oh, we're very cultured," replied Chris. "We act, we sing, we look at pictures."

She was about to stick her toe over the line. "It was finding out that the artist was local that got us so interested," I said quickly. I paused, then added, "Is that why you're here?" I tried to ask the question in a way that wouldn't offend her.

"I'm here because I'm preparing a paper on the museum's Fletcher collection. The work of Cornelius Fletcher is my specialty."

"Oh," I said, feeling a little silly.

"Would you like to know a little about these pictures?" she asked. She sounded friendlier, which I thought might have something to do with the fact that she was slipping into her teacher role. Ever notice that people love to tell you what they know?

"Sure," Chris said. "We're always ready for a little culture."

If I could have kicked her without Ms. Bond's seeing, I would have.

"Let's start with this one," Ms. Bond said, leading us to a large picture that hung just to the right of the door. "It's called 'Love and Flowers.'"

"Hey, I like this!" I said in surprise. "It's sure prettier than 'Early Harvest.'"

Ms. Bond gave me her "What a rude sound!" look. "It's an inferior painting," she said, as if I were some kind of moron not to have known that. "The museum keeps it out for historical purposes, so people can see the growth in Fletcher's work. Other than that, it has little to recommend it. It's shallow and sentimental, pretty much representative of the worst of American art during that period."

I stared at the picture, which showed a woman and a little girl playing in a field of flowers.

"I still like it," I muttered to myself.

"Now this piece is from Fletcher's sketchbook," Ms. Bond said, pointing to a pencil drawing of a soldier leaning over a ragged, skinny boy. "He made it while in France, during the war. Notice that the style is cleaner, less cluttered. Of course, it's still sentimental. But he'll get past that."

She showed us several more sketches. The work seemed to get progressively more dark and ugly, which Ms. Bond seemed to think made it progressively more artistic.

"I like the sentimental ones," I said at last.

Ms. Bond sighed. "Most young people do. I suppose as decoration they're quite nice. But they have very little personal vision in them. In the later work you see a man being forced to face a terrible truth, and sharing that truth through his art. Cornelius Fletcher went to war filled with foolish ideas about glory. His later pictures show what he found instead."

After the series of sketches we saw a big painting of a battle scene. Unlike looking at "Early Harvest," where the horror was hidden at first, seeing this picture was like getting hit between the eyes with a hammer.

"This was Fletcher's first major painting after his return from the war," Ms. Bond said. "It doesn't have the subtlety of his later work. Still, it made his reputation."

After I had studied that picture, and the ones that followed it, I said, "It's hard to believe these were painted by the same man who did 'Love and Flowers.'"

I wanted to ask what had happened to change him so much. But I remembered the way Carla Bond had reacted to my curiosity on Saturday, so I let the question hang.

Either Chris had forgotten the woman's snappishness or she didn't care, because she asked, "Is it true that he went mad?"

I waited for Ms. Bond to blast her with one of those looks, but she just nodded. "Quite mad," she said softly.

I decided she must have considered my Saturday questions pure nosiness. Now that Chris and I were trying to get some culture, curiosity was all right.

"Was it because he lost his legs?" pressed Chris.

Ms. Bond looked a little startled. "You two *have* been busy, haven't you?"

I was afraid Chris was going to get smart-alecky again, but she just said, "We learned about it in the library."

Ms. Bond relaxed a little. "Well, I can only approve of such diligent research. Of course, there was much more to it than that. But the family kept the story to themselves. People weren't so public with their tragedies in those days."

"But you know what happened, don't you?" persisted Chris.

She had pressed too far. "Whatever happened, it was long ago," snapped Ms. Bond. "If the family didn't want it talked about, I don't see that people need to dig it up now."

That was pretty much the end of our conversation with Carla Bond. Chris blushed a little, Ms. Bond calmed down a bit, we talked some and then got out of there as quickly as we could.

It was almost time to meet my father anyway. The quickest way to our meeting point was back across Columbus Circle.

Since we had a few minutes and since it was only a week or so after Columbus Day, we stopped to take a look at the statue. While I was staring at it someone grabbed my arm from behind.

I felt a surge of panic. "Hey!" I said, trying to pull free.

"Listen, missy," hissed a scratchy voice. "People who hang around with artists have to be careful!"

CHAPTER TEN

Dark Vision

Yanking my arm free, I spun around. I found myself face to face with a skinny old man who had stringy hair, bad teeth and about two days' worth of gray stubble on his chin.

Before I could say anything, Chris shouted, "You leave her alone!" I could tell she was ready to kick the old guy.

"Wait, Chris," I said. "It's okay. I know him."

"You *know* this guy?"

"I see him on Saturday sometimes," I said. "Don't I, Jimmy?"

"That's right, missy," he wheezed. "Saturdays. But *I* seen *you* this Saturday. Yes, I did. You, too," he added, pointing to Chris. "You were up to the Watson place. You want to be careful when you go up there."

"Why?" I asked. "Why do we need to be careful, Jimmy?"

"There's something terrible up there." Shaking his head, he backed away from me. "Something terrible, something wonderful. And folks who hang around up there best be careful."

"What is it, Jimmy? What's in the house?"

The old man's eyes got big, and he put his finger on his lips. "Never did tell," he whispered, "never will tell. What kind of a guy do you think I am?"

"Jimmy!"

"Never did tell, never will tell," he repeated. Then he turned and moved away from us as fast as he could.

Chris started after him.

"Don't bother," I said. "He won't tell us anything now."

"How do you know?"

"I've seen him like this before."

"Well that's another thing I want to know. How come you know that old coot?"

"He comes to the feeding program where Dad and I work."

Chris nodded. I'd been telling her about the program just a few weeks before. One of the downtown churches serves a daily meal for the kinds of people my grandmother used to call down and out. Only now they're called homeless and hungry. Anyway, during the week a professional runs the program. But on weekends it's handled by volunteers from different churches around town. My father and I like to go help when it's our church's turn.

To tell you the truth, I was a little nervous about it the first time I went. But I found I really enjoyed the work. It feels good to do something that helps, even if only a little.

"How can you stand it?" asked Chris with a shudder. "Guys like that give me the creeps."

"He used to scare me until I'd handed him his lunch a few times. Then I realized he's just a lonely old man."

"Lonely and *weird*! What was that all about anyway?"

"You've got me." I was trying not to sound too shaken up. I don't know why, but I felt some odd sense of loyalty to Jimmy. Maybe when you feed someone you start to get attached to him.

Even though I tried to hide it, Jimmy's words had spooked me. What was going on up at Phoebe Watson's house? And what did Jimmy know about it?

"I don't have the slightest idea what this is all about yet," Chris said, as we walked toward the corner where we were supposed to meet my dad.

"That makes two of us. Right now we've got more mystery than we have clues."

"I keep thinking about those shutters," Chris said. "Who—or what—was slamming them?"

"I suppose the main candidate is the little girl in the bed."

"Do you really think so?"

I paused. "No, not really. It's just that she's
the only ghost we saw. Could it have been some
kind of trick? You know, someone trying to scare
Phoebe?"

Chris shrugged. "Possible. But my guess is
that there's another ghost kicking around
Phoebe's house."

"Then we've got two ghosts—"

"Not to mention a mad genius."

"Well, he could be one of the ghosts."

"He probably is. But what does he want?"

"He doesn't want Phoebe to sell the house,
that's for sure. At least, that's what she seems to
think."

Chris paused to stare at a pigeon. "You'd
think he'd be more interested in having her keep
the picture," she said.

"I don't know. If that's the family home, he
might want her to stay there."

"But we don't know if it is the family home,"
Chris said. "Phoebe has a different last name, so
she must have been married at some point."

I nodded. "So the other ghost could be her husband." I sighed. "This is getting too complicated.
We need more information."

Chris tugged at a strand of her reddish hair
and said, "We could just forget the whole thing."

I knew she didn't mean it. We had to go on
with this. Seeing ghosts is special, and it gives us
a special responsibility. I was trying to figure out

how to say that without sounding stupid when my father drove up in the GC.

GC stands for Golden Chariot, which is what my dad calls his car, an ancient yellow and white Cadillac with huge fins. I don't want to say it's overgrown, so let's just say that if cars were dogs, this one would be a Saint Bernard on steroids.

"Expedition successful?" asked Dad, as Chris and I climbed into the front seat, which easily holds all three of us with no crowding.

"Well, we learned a lot," I said. "It just doesn't make much sense yet."

Taking turns, Chris and I filled him in on the information we had picked up from Ms. de la Pena, Marcus, and Ms. Bond. By the time we were finished, we had reached Chris's house.

"Bus stops here," said my dad, pulling up to the curb.

"Call me if you get a flash of inspiration," Chris whispered as she stepped out of the car.

"Okay," I said. "You do the same."

I sighed as she ran up to her front door.

"She's a good kid," said my father.

"I *hate* it that she lives way over here," I replied.

He nodded. He didn't say much as we drove home.

I decided to take a walk before supper. I had a lot to think about. (Besides, I'm trying to keep from putting on weight.)

As I strolled down Westcott Street, I spotted Norma kneeling on the sidewalk, talking a mile a minute. At first I thought she was talking to the ground. As it turned out, she was encouraging some daffodil bulbs she had just planted.

"Now you kids listen," she said, patting the soil. "I'm expecting to see you come spring. So you have a nice sleep, then just bust up and bloom so bright it hurts my eyes. You hear?"

"Do you always talk to the things you plant?" I asked.

Norma shrieked, then turned to look in my direction. "Nine!" she cried, putting her hand on her chest. "For a minute I thought one of those bulbs was talking back to me."

Then she laughed that huge laugh of hers.

"I'm glad you came by," she continued, climbing to her feet. "I was meaning to give you a call. Come on—let's go have a cup of coffee."

I made a face.

Norma made a face back. "I forgot you have unenlightened taste buds. Well, come on up and chat with me while *I* have some."

I followed Norma up the walk to her porch, wondering what she wanted to talk about. We settled onto the swing, where I decided I could easily forgive a coffee addiction in someone who could make the kind of chocolate chip cookies she now handed me.

I felt happy as I looked out on our neighborhood. The sky was filled with dark clouds, but it was so late in the afternoon that the sun was below them, shining in from the side. The light was strong and dramatic, the trees draped in scarlet and orange. The still, quiet air was warm enough to be comfortable, cool enough to feel fresh and exciting.

Norma took a sip of coffee and said, "I have bad news."

I looked at her nervously. "What's wrong?"

"Phoebe Watson is in the hospital."

"What happened?" I cried.

"Heart problem. Fairly mild, I think, but she'll be in for several days. I went to visit her this afternoon. She asked if you would mind going over to her house on a mission of mercy."

"What do you mean?"

"She wants you to take care of General Pershing."

I must have looked blank because Norma laughed and said, "Her cat. Remember? I'd do it myself, only I'm allergic, and Phoebe wants someone to make a fuss over the obnoxious little beast."

I hesitated for a moment. The idea of going back to Phoebe's house by myself was frightening. On the other hand, it was hard to say when either Chris or I would have another chance to visit the place.

"I'd be glad to," I said. "How do I get in?"

"Phoebe keeps a key under a flowerpot on the back porch. The cat food is in the cupboard next to the refrigerator."

I wanted to sit and talk to Norma, but if I was going to feed the cat, I had to get moving. I hurried home to work things out with my father. We decided I would ride my bike over to Phoebe's, and he would come get me about forty-five minutes later.

The reason I was riding my bike *over* was that he was in the middle of cooking supper. The reason he was going to drive me *back* was that he doesn't want me out on the streets alone after dark. He says he's afraid the bogeyman will take me away.

Actually, I know he has good reasons not to want me out after dark. But it makes me mad that I can't walk a mile or so through our own neighborhood by myself.

I thought about calling Chris. But she wouldn't be able to get to my house in time to go with me, so I decided I should just get moving. I knew she would be annoyed that I had done this on my own, but I couldn't figure any way around it. Phoebe had asked me to feed the cat, and it needed to be done that night.

By the time I got my bike to the top of Phoebe's hill, I was panting. The light was almost gone—you could just see the sun setting beyond Phoebe's house. The shadow of the tower stretched toward me like a long finger of darkness. Each of the jagged stones from the broken wall cast a little shadow of its own. I remembered that one of the Fletcher pictures we had seen in the museum was called "Stones Can Break Your Heart."

The flagstone path that led from the street to Phoebe's house was too steep to ride up, so I got off my bike and walked it to the porch, where I discovered that I had forgotten to bring my lock. To be safe, I took the bike around back.

The shrubs and bushes in the backyard were overgrown and tangled. It looked as if it had been years since anyone had really taken care of the place. The yard stretched down the far side of the hill.

I realized how isolated Phoebe's house was.

As I leaned my bike against an old tree, the sun, which had almost set anyway, disappeared behind some clouds. It was getting hard to see.

The wind began to blow harder, swirling the dead leaves around my feet.

Nice setting for a haunted house, I thought.

Back on Norma's porch this trip had seemed like a good idea. Now I wasn't so certain. It suddenly hit me that the fact I had never met a ghost who was actually bad didn't mean there was no such thing. And even a ghost that isn't nasty is pretty scary when you're on your own.

It's interesting how you can explain to yourself all the reasons why you shouldn't be scared, and have your body completely ignore the fact. I could feel my stomach start to twist. The hairs at the back of my neck were beginning to prickle. And I hadn't even gone inside yet.

I found the key and unlocked the door. As I turned the knob, the storm began.

CHAPTER ELEVEN

Footsteps in the Dark

Lightning ripped across the sky. Raindrops exploded around me, pelting down so hard you would have thought they were coming from guns instead of clouds. I dashed inside and slammed the door shut to get away from them. I stood in pitch darkness, the rain racket making me feel as if I were trapped inside a drum.

Suddenly I felt something rub against my leg. I jumped and yelled, then laughed when I realized it was only the cat that I had come to feed.

"You lonely, kiddo?" I asked, scooping the mass of black and white fur off the floor.

General Pershing opened his mouth and hissed at me.

"Great," I said. "You ought to meet my cat. You have a lot in common."

I dropped the general and felt around for the light switch.

Rain continued to pound against the windows.

With the lights on I quickly found the cat food, right where Norma had said it would be. I tried to make a fuss over General Pershing, but he was far more interested in his meal than in me. It was clear I would have to wait until he had finished eating to give him the attention Phoebe wanted him to have.

I decided to go into the parlor and look at "Early Harvest."

I suppose that sounds kind of dumb. I mean, I've already told you how much I hated the thing. So why was I going back to look at it again? I don't know. Maybe it was the same kind of thing that makes people stop to look at accidents—or watch the evening news, for that matter.

I switched on the parlor light, then crossed to the fireplace. Resting my hands on the mantelpiece, I stared at the picture.

A streak of lightning sizzled through the night.

Thunder shook the house.

I swallowed. As before, I could feel myself being drawn into the picture. The storm made it seem even more real than it had seemed the first time. In my head, the booming of the thunder became the roar of cannons. Once again the smell of smoke and blood seemed to fill my nostrils.

I staggered forward and felt a branch lash against my face.

Nearby a dying man cried out. He reached for me, begging me to save him. As I stepped closer, he moaned and closed his hand around my ankle.

I screamed—and found myself back in Phoebe Watson's parlor, trembling like a stretched rubber band that's just been plucked. I closed my eyes and rubbed my hands over my face.

Had I actually stepped into the painting?

Was I somehow slipping into the past?

Or was I just losing my mind?

Before I could decide, I heard a new sound. Not the wind and the rain. Not the crash of thunder. Not the cat. Just a small voice, crying out somewhere above me.

A human voice, a little girl, crying out in a house that was empty except for General Pershing and me.

A shiver rippled through me. I had to get out of there!

I started for the door and then stopped.

"What are you so afraid of, Nine?" I whispered to myself. "You know who that voice belongs to. It's just a little kid—a lonely little girl, crying in her bed."

All right—so it was a dead kid. She was still lonely.

Even so, I doubt that I could have done what I did next, if not for my previous experiences with ghosts.

Taking a deep breath, I headed for the stairs—and the waiting ghost.

Again I found the light switch. I flicked it on, partly because I wanted the light and partly, I'll confess, because I thought it might make the ghost disappear. However, the single dim light that appeared at the top of the stairs wasn't apt to frighten away any spirit that wanted to be heard.

Putting my right hand against the peeling wallpaper, I started up the stairs.

"Daddy!" cried the voice. "Daddy, where are you?"

A lump was starting to form in my throat. Not a scared lump; a sad lump. I took another step.

Thunder shook the house.

I continued to climb. At the top of the stairs, I turned right and headed for the tower room.

The door was open.

The shaft of light that stretched across the floor didn't quite reach the big brass bed. It didn't matter—pale and colorless as they are, ghosts seem to have some internal light of their own. I could see the little girl more clearly this time. She was huddled in the covers. She looked miserable and lonely.

What could I do for her? I certainly couldn't get her daddy. I didn't even know for sure who he was.

Besides, I had a feeling that whoever he might have been, he was long dead himself by now.

Lightning sizzled and snapped through the air outside. During the long crash of thunder that followed, the light flickered and then went out.

I stood in the darkness, not daring to move.

I don't think darkness makes any difference to ghosts. At least, the little girl in the bed didn't seem to notice the change. As I watched, she got to her knees. Crawling to the foot of the bed, she grabbed the knob that topped one of the bedposts and tried to turn it.

Nothing happened.

After a while she lay back down and stared at the ceiling, tears rolling down her cheeks.

I didn't know what to do. I wished I had some sort of manual I could read, something that provided advice on dealing with different kinds of ghosts.

While I stood, staring, the ghost slowly faded out of sight.

I took a deep breath and sighed. My sense of relief didn't last long; seconds later I heard something moving downstairs. At first I thought it was the cat. I wouldn't even have minded if it was another ghost. But ghosts don't stumble and curse.

Someone else was in the house.

For an instant I hoped it might be my father. But he wasn't due for another twenty minutes, and we had agreed that he would honk for me when he got there. So he wouldn't be in the house.

But if it wasn't him, then who was it?

I held my breath. I could hear the intruder, whoever it was, walking along the downstairs hall.

Then the footsteps started up the stairway.

CHAPTER TWELVE

Dumb Waiting

I had to hide someplace. But the only thing left in the room was the ghost's bed. I was more than willing to help the ghost who slept in it; I wasn't sure I could bring myself to hide underneath it.

Even so, I might have had to—if I hadn't remembered the dumbwaiter.

I slid across the floor without lifting my feet, then groped around on the dark wall, searching for the little door.

The footsteps had reached the top of the stairs. There was a moment of silence. Then I saw the beam of a flashlight sweep up and down the hallway.

Finally I found the dumbwaiter door. I fumbled with the latch. The door swung open. I paused to listen.

Whoever was in the hall was coming toward the tower room.

I had no choice. Climbing into the dumbwaiter, I scrunched up as small as I could. Then I used my fingertips to pull the door most of the way shut.

The intruder stepped into the room. "Who's there?" asked a gruff male voice. The flashlight beam swept across the walls. Holding my breath, I pulled the door the rest of the way shut. Then I pressed my head against my knees and hoped the pounding of my heart wouldn't give me away.

After a few moments I heard the man leave the room. I thought I was safe—until the dumbwaiter started to move.

I choked back a cry of fright.

If I was scared when the dumbwaiter started to move, I was even more so when it stopped. I mean, how would *you* like to be trapped in a box in a wall in a haunted house in the middle of a storm while a prowler roamed the halls looking for you?

It was not, shall we say, the best moment of my life. In fact, I was pretty much convinced I was going to die.

Having met a few ghosts, I'm not as scared of dying as some people I know. After all, I have pretty good evidence that dying isn't the end of everything. On the other hand, I still have things I want to do in this lifetime. So as far as I'm concerned, I am much too young to take the Big Dirt Nap.

I began to wonder just how long my air was going to last. After a few seconds I decided that given the construction of the shaft, air could probably get to me.

Food and water, on the other hand, could not.

What did that mean?

I wasn't sure. After all, it's not easy to work things through when your brain is screaming, "JUST GET ME OUTTA HERE!"

Suddenly I became aware that my first problem wasn't going to be air *or* water. It was going to be cramps. My body was realizing it had not been designed to be stuffed into a tiny box. My legs started to complain, and I had a pretty good idea that the feeling was going to get worse, fast.

Suddenly the thing I wanted most in the whole world was to be able to stretch.

I began to wonder if you could die from muscle spasms.

Think! I commanded myself. *And not about dying, stupid.* All right—what else was going to happen?

Well, my father would be there in a while. He would park outside. He would honk. When I didn't come out, he would come to the door. It would be locked. He would yell. No one would answer. He might go around back. The door was unlocked, so he would come in. So far, so good—except there was someone else in the house.

A horrible thought hit me. What if the intruder was carrying a gun?

I swallowed hard. This was like planning a chess game: You make a move, which causes your opponent to make a move. Now you've got choices—and each choice creates more possibilities. All of a sudden your brain is frying. For example, would Dad's arrival scare away the intruder—or would it get him shot?

I had to get out of there!

Finally I did the only thing I could think of, which was to jump. That may sound silly—I mean, you can't really jump when you're scrunched up inside a little box. The movement I made was more like a heavy-duty twitch—up, then down.

To make things trickier, I was trying to do it without making any noise. On my fifth bounce the dumbwaiter started to move. Unfortunately, the movement lasted less than second. I think I managed to go about an inch and a half.

Well, it was a start.

I bounced again.

Another inch.

A bounce, an inch, a bounce, an inch, a bounce—and suddenly the dumbwaiter broke loose, and I went plunging down the inside of the wall.

I buried my scream against my knees—which were still only about a quarter of an inch from my face.

I don't know what my fall sounded like from the outside, but from where I was, the noise was appalling.

I was terrified. But my fear didn't last long; it took only a few seconds for me to hit bottom.

I landed with a thump that made me bite my tongue. I could taste blood. Suddenly I heard a slithering noise above me—the broken rope coiling down on top of the dumbwaiter.

I hesitated. Should I get out and make a run for it? Or stay here and hope the intruder wouldn't be able to figure out where the noise had come from?

If I was lucky, I might even have scared whoever it was away. On the other hand, if the intruder did decide to investigate, I'd rather be out of the dumbwaiter than in it. I didn't like the image that flashed through my head of someone throwing open the door and shining a light in my face.

I liked even less the thought of what might happen next.

I pushed on the door—softly, with the hope that it wouldn't make any noise.

To my relief, it swung open without a sound.

I figured I was in the kitchen—that was the only place it made sense for the dumbwaiter to have landed. So the odds were good that I could find plenty of places to hide if my unknown friend decided to show up. Even better, maybe I could get to the door and get out.

Taking a deep breath, I stretched my right leg down to the floor. No sooner had I found solid footing than General Pershing decided to rub against my ankle. I thought I was going to have a heart attack right then.

Trying not to step on the cat's tail, I finally got both feet on the floor. My legs began to wake up, which meant that I had a pincushion attack. I ignored it and tried to figure out exactly where I was. The power was still out, but a flash of lightning showed me the door. Thank goodness!

Working slowly, trying to be silent, I groped my way across the floor. It was a little early for my father to be there. But I figured it was better to wait outside and get drenched than to wait inside and get killed.

As I was feeling around for the doorknob, I heard a new sound. It was very soft, so low that I wouldn't have heard it had there not been a momentary lull in the storm.

It was the sound of someone singing.

Only this didn't come from upstairs—I was too far away for that. It came from the cellar.

"'Over there,'" sang the voice. "'Over there. We'll be over, we're going over, and we won't come back till—'"

A new burst of rain drowned out the rest of the sound. Even though the words were muffled, the voice seemed oddly familiar.

What was going on here?

I wasn't sure I wanted to know. Finding the doorknob, I turned it softly and then stepped out into the rain.

I thought the excitement was finally over—until I looked up and saw the ghost of Cornelius Fletcher floating in front of me.

CHAPTER THIRTEEN

In the Gazebo

Fletcher's ghost was sort of standing in the rain. I say "sort of" for two reasons.

First, I'm not sure he was really *in* the rain. Water was pouring down all around him, but he didn't look a bit wet. Of course, maybe ghosts don't get wet. What I really wondered about was the rain that was landing *on* him. I didn't see it going through his misty form, but I didn't see it running off either. I have no idea where it was going.

The second reason I say "sort of" is that I'm not sure he was really standing. The image of the ghost was clear from the top of its head to its waist. Below that it began to fade. From the knees down you could barely see him at all.

It was those misty, almost-gone legs, eerie re-minders of a distant tragedy, that convinced me this was the ghost of Cornelius Fletcher.

His lean face was filled with despair; his large, dark eyes looked like holes into another world. His hair was long, but I couldn't tell what color it had been. He had a straight nose and a square, outthrust jaw. He was a good-looking man, or would have been, if not for the sorrow and anger that twisted his features.

We stared at each other for a moment. Then he turned and began to drift across the yard. I followed him.

The rain hit me hard, and in seconds my clothes were clinging to my skin. I had gone about ten feet when a sheet of lightning rippled through the sky. In the instant of light the ghost nearly disappeared. Then the darkness returned, and his image grew sharp once more.

The thunder that followed the lightning made me jump. Before the sound had faded, another flash of lightning neoned through the sky. The ghost ignored it, continuing to drift across the lawn.

"Where are we going?" I called.

No answer—not that I really expected one. None of the ghosts Chris and I had met so far had ever talked to us. I had no reason to think this one would be any different.

If the two of us continue to become more sensitive to the spirit world, I hope that will change. Our work would be a lot easier if ghosts could just tell us what they want!

The rain was coming down so hard now that it was becoming difficult for me to see him.

"Where are we going?" I shouted in frustration.

No answer but the pounding of the rain.

As we continued down the hill, another flash of lightning lit up the night. I could see a small white structure ahead of us. The rain was so thick that it wasn't until we got closer that I could tell it was a summerhouse—a gazebo, as my father would say.

The ghost led me inside.

I was relieved to be out of the rain—though only slightly, since I was already so soaked that the only real improvement came from the fact that the rain was no longer actually beating against me. I had to be careful where I stood to maintain that situation, since the roof leaked, and in several places the water was drizzling through it in steady streams. I also had to be careful because of the spongy condition of the wooden floor, which had rotted right through in some spots. I had a feeling the leaking had been going on for years.

Now that we were out of the rain, what I really wanted to do was ask the ghost some questions. I certainly had enough of them, such as, "Why did you bring me here?" and "Are you the one who was banging the shutters?" and "If so, why?" and "Is it true that you don't want Phoebe to sell the house?" and "If not, why not?" and "Who is the little girl upstairs?" and "Who was singing in the cellar?"

Of course, I would have settled for just asking, "What's going on around here anyway?"

Not that I thought I would get any answer.

A streak of lightning sizzled down nearby. The clap of thunder that followed less than a second later was so powerful it nearly knocked me over. I shook my head and tried to sort through the images my eye had picked up in the instant of illumination.

The gazebo was built like the tower room, with many short, flat sides joining to make a nearly circular shape. From the center of the ceiling hung an old-fashioned swing like the one Norma had on her porch. One side of it had come unhooked and was dragging on the ground.

Cornelius Fletcher drifted past the broken swing to the far side of the little building. He stopped next to a bench that looked something like a window seat and pointed to it.

I crossed the floor, feeling my way around the swing. As I got closer, I expected the ghost to do a quick fade, but he continued to float there, waiting for me.

I slowed down. I may be used to ghosts, but I wasn't used to getting this close to them. At least, not voluntarily.

Fletcher looked impatient.

As I took another step forward, I heard a car horn honk from the direction of the house.

My father! He was here to pick me up. And since he was honking, he'd probably already been waiting for a few minutes.

Normally I wouldn't mind making him wait. But I was afraid he might get impatient and go up to the house. If the prowler was carrying a gun, I sure didn't want Dad to go to the door and startle him into using it.

I had to get back to the car.

But the ghost clearly wanted me to find something.

Honk! Honk!

"Sorry," I said to the ghost. "I've got to get out of here."

I turned to go. As I did, the broken side of the swing lifted into the air. Floating back to the ceiling, it pressed itself into place.

The swing began to rock, slowly at first, then faster and harder than it ever could have moved with people in it. In seconds it was whizzing back and forth so violently that I knew if I tried to walk past it, I would be knocked flat.

I spun back to the ghost. "What do you want?" I screamed.

Again he pointed to the window seat.

I raced across the floor and threw open the top of the seat. In the faint glow that came from Cornelius Fletcher, I could just make out the clutter that filled the seat: moldy blankets, chipped dishes, a croquet set.

The car horn sounded again. I had to get out of there!

I glanced over my shoulder. The swing was still whizzing back and forth.

I stared at the contents of the bench in dismay. I didn't have time to go through all this stuff. I had to get to the car before my father decided to go into the house to get me.

I turned toward the ghost and screamed, "What do you want me to take?"

Cornelius Fletcher scowled. Lightning blazed through the sky. Then a metal box rose slowly out of the seat, until it was floating just before my face.

CHAPTER FOURTEEN

Fatherly Concerns

I hesitated for a second, then reached forward and snatched the box out of the air.

Instantly the ghost disappeared. Behind me I heard a clatter as the broken side of the swing dropped to the floor.

Honk! Honk!

"I'm coming!" I screamed as I stumbled over the spongy wooden floor and back into the rain. Clutching the box to my chest, I raced up the hill. Twice I slipped on the wet grass and fell. The second time, the corner of the box poked me in the stomach, knocking my breath away.

The cold rain lashed me. My soaking clothes made it hard to run. My hair stuck to my head as if it had been painted on.

At the top of the hill, I headed for my bike, then veered away. I didn't want to waste the five or ten seconds it would take to grab my wheels. I was too worried about my father's going up to the

house. I shot around the front corner just in time
to see him getting out of the car.

"Let's go!" I cried.

I raced down the sidewalk and scrambled into
the Golden Chariot.

My father was glad enough to get out of the
rain. But he wasn't too pleased about the situation
in general. After he started the car, he turned to
me and snapped, "What in heaven's name were
you doing all this time?"

"Give me a minute," I said. I was clutching
the spot where the box had jabbed me. It really
hurt.

Dad turned on the ceiling light. "Are you all
right?" he asked. The anger had vanished from his
voice.

"I'm okay. Let's just go home. *Please*. I promise I'll tell you all about it after we get there."

Then I realized there was one more thing I
had to do first. "Is there a phone between here and
home?"

"I don't think so. Why?"

So much for waiting until we got home to explain things.

"There's a prowler in Phoebe's house. We have
to call the police right away."

"Well, why didn't you say so?"

The truth was, until that moment I had been
so worried about getting the two of us away from
harm that it hadn't occurred to me. But we had

to get someone to the house fast! For all we knew, the prowler was looting Phoebe's house while we talked.

"Dad!" I said urgently.

He nodded, revved the car, and off we drove. It was a lot faster by car than by bike, especially the way my father was driving now, so in less than three minutes I was running up the steps of our house to make my call. The drive had kept him pretty occupied, and as soon as he got in the house, he had to get on the phone to assure the police that this was no prank. So it wasn't until he hung up the phone that he had a chance to turn to me and say, "All right, spill. What went on over there?"

I started to answer. But now that the crisis was past, everything started to hit me. I was wet and cold and frightened, and when I tried to speak, my teeth began to chatter.

My dad closed his eyes. "Save it," he said. "First thing you do is get out of those wet things and into a hot shower."

"Th-th-that's a g-g-good idea," I said, rubbing my arms to try to warm them.

"Then," he said, "you owe me a story!"

I nodded and headed up the stairway, which was now completely stripped of wallpaper. As I peeled myself out of my soaking clothes, I replayed in my mind everything that had just happened. I was dying to know what the ghost wanted—but at

least now we had some kind of a clue. I couldn't
wait to open that box and see what was inside.

I turned the shower up as hot as I could stand
it. I was cold down to my bones, and the steaming
water running over my skin made me feel as if I
were taking a short trip to heaven.

While I toweled down, I began to wonder
about the person wandering around in Phoebe's
house. Was this just a typical robbery—or was the
break-in somehow connected to whatever else was
going on up there? I wondered if the prowler was
trying to steal her picture!

After wrapping myself in my robe, I slipped
into my Garfield slippers, grabbed the metal box
Cornelius Fletcher had shown me, and clomped
down the stairs. My dad was sitting in the dining
room, looking through a book of wallpaper sam-
ples.

The table was set for dinner. Standing in the
center was a big tureen of soup and a plateful of
Dad's special homemade biscuits. A curl of steam
rose from the pot of herbal tea sitting beside my
plate.

I smiled. I had been through so much, I had
forgotten he'd been making dinner when I left for
Phoebe's house.

"What do you think of this?" he asked, holding up the book to show me a page of red-and-gold
striped wallpaper.

I stuck out my tongue and wrinkled my nose.

"That's the trouble with wallpaper," he said. "If you have more than one person living in the house, it's almost impossible to find a pattern everybody likes."

He closed the book and nodded toward the table. "Madame may have her dinner now if she wishes."

"Madame wishes," I said, sitting down and pouring myself some tea. I put my hands over the steaming cup. Even after my shower the warmth felt good.

"So," said my dad, splitting a biscuit and slathering it with butter. "What's in the box?"

"You've got me," I said, shrugging. "I won't know until we open it. All I know is that the ghost really wanted me to take it."

My father raised an eyebrow. "The ghost in the tower?"

I shook my head. "The ghost outside. I think it's Cornelius Fletcher."

He made a little choking sound. "*You met Cornelius Fletcher?*" he asked in astonishment.

"Well, it's hard to say for sure, since he didn't talk to me. But I'm pretty certain."

"Why don't you start at the beginning," he said. He stood up and ladled out the soup. Then he sat down and folded his hands. "I'm all ears."

"That's going to make it hard to eat your soup."

"I'll pretend I didn't hear that," he said calmly, "if you will just get on with your story."

When I was done, I realized that he was staring at me with a really unhappy expression. "You could have been killed," he said, speaking slowly.

"Do you think I don't know that?"

"Nine, you've got to start being more careful." He paused. "Not just you. *I*'ve got to stop letting you do stuff like this." He took a deep breath, and I could tell he was about to wallow in guilt.

I put down the spoonful of soup I had been lifting to my lips. "Whoa, Dad," I said. "Calm down. What did you let me do that was so terrible? It's not like I was out walking the streets at midnight. I was helping a friend. Who could figure someone would break in to her house at this time of day?"

He stared into his soup. I could tell he was really upset by what had happened. But he knew I was right: It hadn't happened because I had done anything unusual. It just happened.

I do think it's interesting that the thing we were both worried about was the prowler, and not the ghost.

Finally he heaved a deep sigh. "I don't want anything to happen to you. But you're right—you weren't doing anything out of the ordinary. For that matter, I know you could get run over by some insane driver while you're walking to school tomorrow. Sometimes I wish you were tiny again, so I could just keep you here and keep you safe."

I made a face.

He laughed. "Sorry, but that's the way fathers feel. Mothers, too, I suppose. Listen, sweetheart, you can't understand how much I want to keep you safe. But I know there's no point in keeping you locked in the house. That's not safe for your spirit. I just—oh, I don't know."

He put down his spoon and walked into the kitchen. I waited a few seconds, then followed him.

"Dad?"

He put his arms around me. "I love you, Nine," he said, holding me close.

I hugged him back. "I love you, too, Dad."

We stood like that for a minute, and it made me think of the ghost in Phoebe Watson's house— the one who kept crying for her daddy. I hugged *my* father a little tighter. Then I said, "Let's find out what's in that box."

He nodded.

But when we went back to the dining room and put it on the table, I hesitated. "You know, Chris should really be here for this."

He sighed. I doubt he would have agreed to it if he hadn't been feeling so mushy, but he told me to call Chris. He said that if her parents agreed, he would drive over to pick her up.

Between getting Chris and telling her everything that had happened, it was over an hour before we were ready to try again. Finally the three of us—Dad, Chris, and I—sat down around the table.

"Ready?" I asked.

"Ready," they said.

I pulled the box toward me, then pressed the latch.

CHAPTER FIFTEEN

"This Is a House of Darkness"

To my dismay, the box wouldn't open.

"Let me see," said my father, after watching me struggle with it for a few moments.

I passed the box to him.

He looked it over and said, "It's rusted shut. I'll be right back."

After he had dashed down to the cellar, Chris turned to me. "I can't believe you went to Phoebe's house without me!"

"What was I supposed to do? Drive over and get you?"

"You weren't supposed to do anything. It just makes me mad. Not at you. Just mad. I wish kids could drive!"

"Now that," said my father, coming into the room with a handful of tools and bottles, "is perhaps the most frightening idea in what has already been a long, frightening night. Nine, go get some old newspapers, will you?"

We spread the papers on the table. Dad squirted some stuff into the hinges and the latch area of the box, then began tapping at them with a tiny pointed tool. He sticks his tongue out when he's concentrating; at one point he was concentrating so hard, I was afraid he was going to bite it off. Finally he whispered, "Come on, come on, that's the way!"

When the latch came free, he smiled and turned out his hands, like a waiter presenting a meal in a fancy restaurant. I could tell he felt smug about getting the box open. He was also saying that now it was my turn.

I opened the box. Inside lay a packet of letters, tied together with a faded red ribbon. Underneath the packet were some loose envelopes and some scraps of paper.

I took out the packet first.

My hands shook a little as I untied the ribbon. "They're all to Amanda Fletcher," I said after a moment. "The address is the same as Phoebe's house."

I took out the first letter and unfolded it. The paper was worn, the ink faded. But the handwriting was beautiful, an odd combination of cursive and printing. Some of the letters were formed in a way I had never seen before. Even so, they were clear and easy to read.

"An artist's handwriting," said my father when I showed it to him.

"Read it aloud," Chris said.

I cleared my throat and began. This is what it said:

March 23, 1918
Somewhere in France

My Dearest Amanda,

It is raining, and the entire world seems to be made of mud.

In the distance I hear the boom of cannons as the bombardment continues.

The trench in which I sit is seven feet deep and a yard wide. It runs north and south for nearly a quarter of a mile, our own little world below ground, where we lurk while we wait for the Hun to attack—or for the orders that will send us once more to attack him.

These trenches cut across most of northern Europe now, as if the devil himself had plowed the fields with a finger of fire.

A few feet from me lies a man who is dying. He was wounded this morning, but there has been no way to get him medical attention. The stub of his arm, which was blown away at the elbow, is bound with a strip torn from my shirt.

I find I like to tend the wounded, though I have little enough skill at it.

Oh, Amanda, you and Alida are ever on my mind. I long to see you, touch you, hear your voices. I need to remember goodness, for it seems to me now as if the entire world has gone bad. Or maybe only mad, for what I see all around me are good people doing bad things. As am I.

I do not know if this letter will reach you. I do not know if I will ever reach you. If I do not return, know that I love you, as I have, as I always will. Please kiss Alida for me,

and tell her that her father loves her, too. More than he can
say.

Your husband,
Cornelius

On the back of the second page of the letter
were some sketches Cornelius Fletcher had made
of the things he saw around him. They were pretty
depressing.

The other letters in the packet were all fairly
similar to the first one. But the loose papers in the
box were very different. The most interesting was
a long letter that looked a little like the rough
drafts I write for school: lots of inkblots and
crossed-out lines. It wasn't from Cornelius; it was
from Amanda, to her sister Edith.

Here it is:

December 2, 1920
My Dearest Sister,

How can I find the words to tell you of the tragedy that
has overtaken this house? As if the war, and the wounds Cornelius suffered, were not enough, so many new sorrows have
come to us in the last month that I can hardly bear to write
this. Yet you must know all, for if things here do not change,
I may soon be forced to intrude on you and beg your charity.

I have so much to tell that I scarcely know where to begin. So I shall state the very worst first and then try to explain how all has happened.

Our beloved child, Alida, is dead.

Oh, Edith, how it costs me to write those words. For
even now I do not want to admit that this is true, and writing

it down somehow makes it more real, gives me less chance to pretend it was a dream. Yet if you are to understand my desperate circumstances I must tell you everything.

Here, then, is the story of our tragedy.

As you know, my husband returned from Europe a man much changed. Not only was he nearly crippled by the explosion that maimed his legs. He was changed in spirit. A man once so filled with joy, of such sunny disposition, he was now possessed of the darkest humor. I feel it was not only his physical wounds that caused this damage. In truth, he recognized that he was luckier than many, for unlike those men who could no longer earn their way, he could still paint, even if he could not stand for long periods of time. In these efforts he has had help from the Potter boy.

Though the projects themselves have not been to my liking, I felt they were of help to Cornelius. I hoped that by painting, he could cure the wounds the war had left on his soul, which were deeper and fiercer even than the wounds to his body.

So I watched with sorrow but said nothing as the brush that once gave shape to such sweetness and joy now painted only images that were dark, somber and tragic.

Of all things, only our dear Alida seemed to give Cornelius any joy during these dark days.

Toward the end of November my husband finished a picture he called "Early Harvest." I know this work has greatness in it, but so filled is it with the evil of war that I can scarce stand to look at it.

No sooner was "Early Harvest" done than he began work on a far grander project, one that even now I shudder to remember, and will not describe to you.

"The Lost Masterpiece," whispered Chris.

I looked up, nodded, and went back to reading the letter.

As if all this were not enough, he chose to hurl himself into the political arena—as I imagine you well know, since his drawings appeared in magazines all across the country.

I know that what he has shown in his work is true. But why, why, could he not have let someone else be the one to present that truth?

We fought about this often.

Late in November the influenza struck here, as it did in so many places. There was much panic, and you could see many people walking through the streets with handkerchiefs pressed against their faces to try to ward off the disease.

Sometimes I do believe that ill luck invites more ill luck to join it, for the sickness came to this house. Unwelcome visitor, after the darkness that had already descended upon us! I fell victim to it, as did our dear Alida.

Dr. Dillon phoned a prescription to the pharmacy. As there was no delivery immediately available, Cornelius decided to go for it himself. I lay in my bed, consumed with fever, and he came to me to whisper good-bye. Then he went to Alida's room. Desperately afraid that she would die before he returned, he bent over her bed and whispered, "I am going for medicine to make you well, my dearest. Wait for me. *Wait for me!*"

This I know because he told me of it afterward.

From my bed I could hear the thud of his crutches as he went down the stairs. Then the door closed, and he was gone.

Outside the wind howled, driving the rain against the windows. Alida moaned occasionally, as, I fear, did I, before I finally drifted into a feverish sleep.

I was awakened by a pounding on the front door. I opened my eyes and blinked. The room was light—very light, for during the night the rain had changed to snow, and now the brightness of the sun reflecting off it seemed to flood the room.

So much light for the darkest day of my life.

More pounding at the door. Trembling with fever—and with fear—I drew on my robe and made my way down the stairs. I wondered where Cornelius was and why he had not woken me when he came home.

More pounding. I reached the door and drew it open, leaning against it for support. However, even with the door to support me I could not stand against the terrible sight that greeted me, and I fell to the floor in a faint.

When I woke again, the image I had seen still burned in my brain. That image was of our neighbors from down the hill, Mr. Parker and Mr. Johnson. They stood side by side in my doorway, holding my husband between them. His head, bruised and bloody, lolled forward. His legs hung limply behind him.

Thank God for the kindness of neighbors. While Mr. Parker tended to Cornelius, Mr. Johnson helped me to a chair, where I sat, staring in horror at the sight before me.

"What happened?" I asked when I could finally find voice to speak. But my kindly neighbors did not know, for they had found my husband in this condition only a short time before. It was not until much later that Cornelius was able to tell me that he had been set upon by a gang of thugs who objected to his drawings—set upon, beaten, and left for dead.

Oh, sister, why are men so cruel? Who would beat a man near to death because they disagree with what he has to say?

"I tried to come back," he whispered. "I tried, Amanda. I crawled all the way to the top of the hill. But I could not reach the lock. I could not open the gate. I could not pass the wall."

Nor could he walk, even with his crutches, for his wounded legs had been frozen and were now without life at all.

Oh, sister, it was just as well right then, for in not being able to walk he was not able to climb the stairs. And so it was not he, poor broken man, who had to make the terrible discovery that our daughter had died while he lay freezing outside our gate, clutching her medicine to his chest.

This is a house of darkness. Cornelius has lost his legs—lost them to frostbite and the surgeon's knife. Far worse, he has lost, I fear, his sanity. It is not always so; he has moments when he is lucid. But at other times I know him to be quite mad.

This is why I must think of asking your charity, dear Edith. The truth is, I no longer feel safe here. Alida's spirit seems to haunt the house, though I do not think Cornelius knows this, for he has never been upstairs since that night. His thoughts are absorbed in plans for his horrifying grand project. And I cannot care for myself, or him, as well as I might—for it seems that I am once more with child.

> Your loving sister,
> Amanda Fletcher

CHAPTER SIXTEEN

The Hangman

None of us said anything for a few moments after I read this letter. I could see tears in my father's eyes.

Three letters remained in the pile. These were from Cornelius to Amanda; the first two had been sent to her in care of her sister in Pennsylvania. The first was very short:

January 12, 1921

My Dearest Amanda,
    Please return to me.

Cornelius

The second was longer, but hard to read because some of the words were blurred where the ink had run and smeared, as if drops of water had fallen on the page. Raindrops? Tears? It was impossible to tell.

My Dearest Amanda,

How can I——you what——my heart. There is work——
—must do, a story only I——tell. I do not have the wo——
show what is in me, only the power of my brush——as simple as a quarrel between us. It is something——something
inside me that must be taken out, shown to others. I pray—
—work——to prevent it all from happening again.

Please come home to——miss you more than I can say.
The work——gressing. I have fin——the section on the
east——Start the next——soon.

Come home, come home.

                                        Cornelius

The last letter was not in an envelope. It was
simply folded up. It was very short. All it said was
this:

Dear Amanda,

It is not finished. I cannot finish it. I am defea——

The last word ended with a blot of ink. There
was nothing else on the page or in the box.

When we finished reading the letters, we were
all quiet for a while. What could you say? It was all
so sad, and there wasn't a thing we could do about
it.

At least, not right then. But the fact that the
ghosts were still hanging around indicated that
maybe Chris and I *could* do something. What, I
didn't know. But something.

"Probably the best place to start is with Phoebe Watson," Chris said when we began to discuss it.

"But she's in the hospital."

"That doesn't mean she can't have visitors. In fact, she'd probably like some. Why don't we take her the letters? They really belong to her anyway, and they would make a good way for us to start asking questions."

That sounded like a good plan to me. So after school the next day Chris took a bus over to my house. We had some slopnuggets and milk, then put Cornelius Fletcher's metal box inside a brown bag and started for the hospital. The hospital is connected to the university, so it's an easy walk from my house.

It was a good day for a walk. The air had an October tang, and the sidewalks were littered with gold and scarlet leaves. When we were less than a block from the hospital, I heard a familiar voice say, "Are you being careful?"

"Jimmy!" I cried, spinning around. I was really glad to see him. "Jimmy, what do you know about Cornelius Fletcher?"

Jimmy's eyes went wide. "I hung him," he said.

"You did what?" cried Chris.

"Don't be mad!" said Jimmy desperately. "They were all mad. But I only did what he wanted. I owed him that much!"

"I'm not mad," I said softly. Actually, I felt sick. I hesitated, then asked, "Why did he want you to hang him?"

"Something terrible, something wonderful," whispered Jimmy. "That's what it's all about."

He began to back away from us.

"Wait!" I said.

But he only moved faster. He disappeared into a clump of bushes. By the time we reached it, he was gone.

"How can someone that old move so fast?" asked Chris in astonishment.

"Maybe he didn't move fast so much as move smart."

"Huh?"

I shrugged. "He's been living on the streets for years. He probably knows every hiding place in town."

"Jimmy?" called Chris. "Jimmy, can you hear us?"

No answer.

"Come on," I said. "I doubt he'd tell us anything more even if we found him."

"Okay," muttered Chris. "But I'd like to know what that was all about. Do you think he killed Cornelius?"

"Maybe it was one of those assisted suicide things," I said uneasily. "If you consider everything that had happened to him, it's easy to imagine that Cornelius might decide to end it all. Since he was crippled, maybe he talked Jimmy into helping him."

"But why would Jimmy do it?" asked Chris.

"I don't know!" I said sharply. "Maybe because he's crazy, too!"

But that answer ignored two things. One, we had no reason to think Jimmy had been crazy that far back; two, from what I've been reading lately, it seems that some very sane people have gotten involved in things like that.

We were still discussing Jimmy when we got to Phoebe's room on the third floor of the hospital.

Phoebe looked awful. She had her eyes closed when we walked in, and for a second I thought she was dead. Her skin was so pale, it was almost white. Her hair seemed thin and limp. The lines around her eyes and mouth were deeper than I remembered. I wondered if that was a sign of being in pain.

As we stood there, wondering if we should wake her or just go home, her eyelids fluttered open. When she saw us, she smiled.

"I'm so glad you've come to see me," she whispered, reaching for my hand.

Boy, did that make me feel guilty. After all, we wouldn't have come if not for the letters. Now that I saw what our coming meant to her, I felt like some kind of fake.

"How ya doin', Phoebe?" I asked softly.

She smiled again, although it wasn't really much of a smile. "Better than I look," she said. "Here, give me that button."

She motioned to a little control box attached to a thick cord. Chris handed it to her. Phoebe pushed a button, and the back of the bed began to lift, carrying Phoebe with it.

"That's better," she said, once she was halfway to a sitting position. "Now we can talk. So tell me, how's my baby doing?"

I wondered if she was having hallucinations, until I realized she meant her cat.

"General Pershing is fine," I said.

Phoebe patted my hand. "Norma told me that you were going to feed him. I appreciate it."

I wondered if I should tell her about the prowler in the house. I decided not to; what was the point of giving her something else to worry about right now? But I realized we had better also call the police to see if it looked as if anything had been stolen. It wouldn't be good for her to come home to a ransacked house; that might give her another heart attack.

Chris stepped in to fill the silence I had left. "Nine found something at your house last night. We thought you might like to have it."

Before she could hand Phoebe the box, some-one knocked at the door. It was just a warning; no one expects you to get up and answer the door when you're in the hospital. People just knock. If you say it's okay, they walk in. If you don't say anything, they usually figure you're asleep and walk in to sit beside you. (I got all this from my father, who told me the ground rules we should know if we went to visit Phoebe.)

A warning knock wasn't enough to prepare me for the tall, slender man who stepped into the room. He was extremely handsome. But that wasn't what took my breath away.

It was the fact that I recognized his voice. I had heard it the night before, in Phoebe Watson's house.

I was face to face with the prowler.

CHAPTER SEVENTEEN

Byron

The man who stepped into Phoebe's room was younger than I expected, probably in his early twenties. His thick, golden-brown hair hung down to his wide shoulders. His brown eyes were enormous. With his straight nose and square jaw he was about as gorgeous as a guy can get.

But my heart wasn't pounding so hard because he was handsome. What I was feeling was sheer terror. What was this guy doing here? Had he tracked me down? Had he come to do something bad to Phoebe?

While I was trying to decide whether or not to scream, the newcomer crossed to the bed and said, "Hi, sweetheart. Who are your friends?"

Phoebe grabbed his hand. "Byron!" she cried. "Oh, Byron! I'm so glad you were able to come."

I blinked in confusion. What was going on here?

"It's one of the few advantages of being unemployed," Byron said with a grimace. "You can go where you're needed." He sank into a chair and crossed his long legs.

Phoebe turned her head toward us and said, "Girls, this is Byron Fletcher. He's what we call a shirttail relative."

"Third cousin, I think," said Byron. "Though I usually get that mixed up."

Byron and Phoebe were related? Then what had he been doing prowling around in her house?

"And these are my friends, Nine and Chris," said Phoebe.

"Pleased to meet you," said Byron once we got past the usual explanation about my name. "Are you old friends of Phoebe's?"

"New ones," said Chris.

"Those are good, too," said Byron, smiling.

"How is your work coming, dear?" Phoebe asked.

Byron shrugged. "I like it. Unfortunately, no one seems to think it's worth paying for."

"What do you do?" asked Chris.

I was glad to let her carry the conversation while I tried to figure out what was going on.

Byron smiled. "I'm a starving artist."

"He's trying to carry on the family tradition," said Phoebe, squeezing his hand. "He's good, too— the best since Poppa."

Byron actually blushed. "Phoebe has always been my biggest supporter," he said. "My parents think art is a waste of time. They want me to be a lawyer. They still haven't forgiven me for refusing to go to law school."

"Or me," said Phoebe with a sigh. "They think I encouraged you in your rebellion."

Byron laughed. "You did, you old scoundrel!" He squeezed her hand and winked at me. I thought for a minute that I might fall over.

"When did your train get in?" Phoebe asked.

"Last night," said Byron. He looked troubled. "What a night I had! First, there was this awful storm going on. Then I thought there was a prowler in the house. Only I couldn't find anyone, so I decided it was just my nerves. But just about the time I was settling down, the police showed up, saying they had had a *report* of a prowler."

Chris snorted. I began to blush. This was embarrassing. But since I didn't want Phoebe to get all worried, I figured I'd better straighten things out.

"I sent the police," I said. "I was feeding General Pershing, and when you came in, I thought *you* were a prowler. Actually, what I thought was that I was going to die. I didn't think anyone else was supposed to be there, so I called the police as soon as I got home."

I thought Byron might be angry, but he seemed to find the whole mix-up pretty funny. "It's a good thing Phoebe keeps my picture on her dresser," he said with a laugh. "I had to use it to convince the good officer I really did belong there."

"I'm sorry," Phoebe said. "I didn't think he was coming in from Pennsylvania until today. If I had known he was arriving last night, I wouldn't have bothered you, Nina."

That was just like Phoebe, to call me by my full name.

Byron stood up. "Listen, sweetheart, you seem to be in good hands, and I have some errands to take care of. I'll go now and be back to see you in a little while."

"We can go," I said. I didn't really want to, but it seemed the polite thing to do, since Byron was a relative.

He shook his head. "I really do have some things to take care of. And there's no point in Phoebe's having three visitors now and none later." He bent over and planted a little kiss on Phoebe's forehead. "See you later, sweetness," he said. After winking at Chris and me, he breezed out the door.

Phoebe sighed after he had left. "Poor Byron."

"What's wrong with Byron?" Chris asked.

"He was supposed to get my house. I was going to leave it to him, in my will. I didn't care what he did with it; he could live in it, sell it, rent it—whatever would free him to paint. Only now that won't happen because I have to sell the place to pay my bills. I guess I just lived too long."

"Don't talk like that!" I said fiercely.

Phoebe looked startled, as if she had forgotten we were there. "Oh, it was so nice of you two to come," she repeated, taking my hand again.

"The truth is, we have something to show you," I said. I felt a little less guilty once I confessed that we hadn't come simply out of the goodness of our hearts. (Actually, I think the goodness of my heart still needs a lot of work.)

Chris handed me the bag, and I pulled out the metal box.

"Now this is a surprise," Phoebe said. "I thought you had brought me chocolates. What's inside?"

"Open it and see," said Chris.

Phoebe opened the box. "Oh, my," she murmured after a moment. "Oh, my goodness. Oh, what a treasure! Wherever did you find it?"

I swallowed. "Your father led me to it."

Phoebe's hands began to shake. "My father?" she asked, her voice trembling.

Suddenly I wondered if I was making a mistake by telling her this now. But when I didn't answer right away, Phoebe squeezed my hand with more strength than I would have thought possible. "Tell me!" she said fiercely.

So I told her how the ghost had led me to the gazebo.

"That was Poppa," said Phoebe softly when I was done. "I never saw him, you know," she whispered sadly. "Ever."

While Phoebe took out the letters and began to read them, I tried not to feel guilty for having seen her father. When she got to Amanda's letter, she looked a little surprised. Then she said, "Ah, yes. Mother always wrote her letters at least twice; you can be sure the one that went to Aunt Edith looked *much* better than this. Practically perfect, if you know what I mean."

She read the letter. Tears started to roll down her cheeks. "Such a sad time," she murmured. "Poor Momma. Poor Poppa." She closed her eyes. "Poor everyone."

"We read some of the letters," said Chris.

Phoebe looked a little startled.

"It seemed like the ghost wanted us to," Chris said with a shrug.

Phoebe seemed to accept this explanation. At least, she nodded.

"So what happened next?" asked Chris. "Did your mother go to live with your aunt?"

"For a while. In fact, I was born in Aunt Edith's house. Poppa wrote often, asking Momma to come back. For a long time she wouldn't go. But when I was three, Poppa became very ill. We came home so Momma could care for him."

She paused, and her eyes seemed to look back into the past. "But he was dead before we made it back," she said softly. "I can barely remember it, of course." A tone of horror crept into her voice. "All I remember are the ropes."

"What ropes?" I asked, remembering what Jimmy had said.

Phoebe shook her head. "I don't know," she said. "All I know is that there were ropes everywhere. They scared me. The whole house scared me. I remember screaming."

Her hands began to tremble. I was afraid she was going to die. I took her hand again. It scared me to do that, scared me to think she might die while I was holding her hand. But it was all I could think of to do.

"It's all right," I said. "It's all over, Phoebe."

She looked straight into my eyes. "No, it's not," she whispered. Her hand tightened on mine. "If it were over, Poppa would be gone. But he's still here, and that means that something has been left undone." She closed her eyes and leaned back against the pillow. "Something terrible," she murmured, "something wonderful."

CHAPTER EIGHTEEN

Editorial Comments

"Is she dead?" Chris asked, her voice husky with horror.

I started to pull my hand away. But Phoebe tightened her grip. "Terrible," she whispered, her eyes still closed. "Wonderful."

While I was trying to figure out what to do, Chris found a nurse and dragged her into the room.

The nurse checked Phoebe over, then said, "She's fine—just needs a bit of rest."

Relieved, we tiptoed out of the room.

"Well, now what?" Chris asked, as we left the hospital.

"We go home and make some notes," I said, glancing around nervously. I was afraid Jimmy was ready to jump out at us again. Which reminded me—

"You did recognize that phrase Phoebe used, didn't you?" I asked.

"The bit about 'something terrible, something wonderful'? Yeah, it was the same thing Jimmy said. And I think I know what it means."

"What?"

"The Lost Masterpiece. I think it's still there someplace, and that's why Cornelius doesn't want Phoebe to sell the house."

I gaped at her. "That's brilliant!" I said. "If we could just figure out where it is, it would solve everything."

We went back to my house. But after an hour of writing things down, we weren't much better off than when we had started. We had an idea of what had happened in the past, but no idea how to make things better in the present.

"Well, at least we know what we *want* to do," Chris said, looking at the sheet of paper labeled "How to Help." It had two items listed on it:

(1) Get Cornelius Fletcher and his first daughter back together.
(2) Find the Lost Masterpiece so Phoebe can keep her house.

Unfortunately, we had no idea how to accomplish either of these tasks.

While we were batting ideas back and forth, the phone rang. When I picked it up and said hello, a cheerful voice replied, "So—how's my book coming?"

"Mona!" I cried.

Chris rolled her eyes. I ignored her. Actually, I had been avoiding calling Mona because I knew Chris was still a little jealous about the book. But as long as Mona had called me, I figured we should take advantage of the situation. Mona has made a real study of ghosts, and she might have some ideas that we had missed.

"Your enthusiasm is nice to hear," said Mona. "Does that mean you've written the sample chapters—or are you just trying to keep me in a good mood because you're off schedule?"

"It means I'm glad to hear from you," I said. "Partly because I could use your advice. Chris and I are in the middle of another—situation."

Mona sighed. "I'm going to have to train you to get one adventure written down before you plunge into the next one. But as long as it's in motion, tell me what's happening."

I filled her in on everything that had gone on so far.

"Sounds like it's right up your alley," Mona said. "Tough situation, though. My guess is that the father is stuck outside because he's reliving— you should pardon the pun—the night he couldn't come through for his daughter. Ghosts tend to obsess about that kind of thing. As for the little girl—well, he told her to wait for him, and my guess is that's just what she's doing. Have you checked the bedpost?"

"Huh?"

"You said the little girl was trying to take the top off the bedpost. Have you tried doing the same thing?"

"Agh!" I replied. "I was so frightened that it never occurred to me. Thanks."

"That's what editors are for," Mona said. "Pointing out the things you've missed. But listen—take care of yourself, will you? I don't want my newest author turning into a ghost herself."

"I don't think there's anything to worry about," I said. "After all, the prowler was only Byron, and he had every right to be there."

"True enough," said Mona. "But if this Cornelius Fletcher character is really crazy—and I'd say the man who painted 'Early Harvest' was on the edge—his ghost might be wacky, too. I doubt he can hurt you directly. But if you think about some of the things he's done already, you'll see that there are ways he could harm you without touching you himself. A slamming shutter or a floating box can be a real problem if you're standing too close!"

"But we're on his side!" I protested.

"People don't always recognize their friends," said Mona.

I had a feeling from her tone of voice that she was reminding me of the bratty way I had acted when we first met. But I had only done that because I thought she was after my father. Actually, I still think she's after him, but since she lives three hundred miles away, I don't worry about it too much. And I do have to admit that she's turned out to be a pretty good friend.

"I know what you mean," I said, after a second.

Let her take that however she wanted. I figured if she wanted to use double meanings, I could, too.

"Well," Chris said, after I hung up, "what was that all about?" Her tone was a little sharp.

I filled her in on the conversation. "Mona's right," she said. "Which means that what we have to do now is go back to Phoebe's house and check the bedpost."

"We'll have to wait until Bryon gets back."

"That's okay," said Chris. "I wouldn't mind prowling around a haunted house with a guy who looks like that!"

I smiled. It sounded like a good idea to me. We called the house but got no answer. I figured that Byron was back at the hospital, visiting with Phoebe. Or at least sitting beside her bed. We went downstairs for some more slopnuggets.

My father was home by the time we finally got in touch with Byron. It was just as well; given what had happened the night before, he would not have been amused to find that we had gone back to Phoebe's on our own, even if we had found out that my "prowler" was no real threat.

"I'll go with you this time," he said.

"You're only coming because you hope you'll finally see a ghost yourself," I teased. But frankly, I was just as glad to have him along.

The three of us got into the Golden Chariot and drove to Phoebe's house. As I climbed out of the GC, I noticed again the remains of the stone wall that had once surrounded the property—the wall that had kept Cornelius Fletcher from getting the medicine back to his daughter. I wondered if he had ordered it destroyed after that awful night.

The thought reminded me of something else that had been bothering me. "Dad, can people really die from the flu? I thought it wasn't much more than a bad cold."

"That's pretty much the case these days," he said, "though a stiff case of flu can still be dangerous for someone whose health is already weak. But it used to be a lot worse. Just after World War One there was a pandemic—"

"A what?" asked Chris.

"A pandemic—a worldwide outbreak. If I remember correctly, the death toll was over twenty million."

I looked at him. "That can't be right. We're studying the Holocaust in school right now, and that's three times as many people as died in that."

My dad shrugged. "We remember the Holocaust because it was man-made and based on prejudice. The influenza pandemic was an equal opportunity killer. And we've pretty much beat the flu. I wish I could say the same thing about prejudice."

We had nearly reached the porch by this point. "You know, I've always wanted to see the inside of this place," said my father, interrupting my thoughts about twenty million people.

"Don't get too excited," Chris said. "It's not all that hot."

"Only eleven, and she's lost her sense of wonder," said my father sadly.

Chris was winding up for an answering shot when we reached the door. If we had been waiting for Phoebe, she would have had time to make a whole speech after we rang the bell. But Byron was there in a matter of seconds.

"Come on in," he said, stepping back and holding the door wide.

"Sorry about sending the police over here last night," said my father after we had introduced him.

Byron smiled. "It was reasonable, under the circumstances. I'm sorry I gave you such a scare— though to tell you the truth, you had *me* pretty frightened, too."

After a little talk about how Phoebe was doing, Byron said, "What can I do to help you?"

"Actually, we were hoping to help *you*," said Chris.

"That would be nice. Right now I feel as if I need all the help I can get."

"Then would you mind if we check one of the bedposts upstairs?"

Byron looked startled. "Any particular reason why?"

I took a deep breath and started to explain about the ghost. I was a little worried that he might decide we were all crazy and throw us out. But he just smiled and said, "Phoebe always told me she suspected this place was haunted. I must say, I think it's a little rude of the ghosts to show themselves to strangers and not family members."

"Don't let it bother you," my father said. "I never get to see them either."

He didn't have any better luck this time, although the ghost was there.

She seemed to ignore us as we entered the room. It wasn't until I started to turn the knob on top of the bedpost that she got upset. Then she threw herself at me, hitting and scratching like a wild woman.

CHAPTER NINETEEN

Sketches

When the ghost of Alida Fletcher began to hit and slap at me, I stumbled back, crying out in shock.

Chris grabbed me. "Are you all right?" she asked, her voice trembling.

I nodded. Since Alida's hands had passed right through me, the attack hadn't hurt. But I had felt a terrible coldness when they touched my skin.

My father knelt beside me. "What happened?" he asked, taking me in his arms. His voice was shaking. "Nine, what happened? Are you all right?"

"I'm fine," I said, "Just a little scared."

"What is going on here?" asked Byron. He sounded totally mystified.

"The girl in the bed didn't like what I was doing."

"What girl?"

"She's a ghost," Chris said. "We think she's Phoebe's sister."

Byron stared at us for a moment. "If Phoebe hadn't spent years telling me this place was haunted, I'd say you were crazy and throw you out," he said at last. "But since she did, I guess I'll have to take you seriously." He paused, then added, "But why did the ghost attack you?"

"I'm not sure," I said. "My guess is that she's trying to guard what's in the bedpost."

My father looked around nervously. "Is she still here?"

"She sure is," said Chris.

When Dad looked at me, I nodded in confirmation. What I didn't mention was that she was calling, "Daddy? Daddy, where are you?"

"You try, Mr. Tanleven," Chris said.

"What?"

"Well, you can't see the ghost, so I figure you might not *feel* her either."

My father turned to Byron. "It's up to you. Do you want me to give it a try?"

Byron nodded. "I think we need to find out what's in that bedpost."

My father swallowed, then walked to the bed. "My big chance," he muttered to himself as he reached for the knob.

The moment he touched it the ghost began to flail at him.

He heard me catch my breath. "This is weird," he said, closing his eyes and shivering.

It *was* weird. Alida kept hitting him, trying to drive him away from the bedpost. But since he couldn't see or feel her, she was having no effect on him.

Even if *he* couldn't see her, the scene was starting to drive *me* crazy. "Stop!" I cried at last. "You leave him alone. He's not going to hurt anything. We only want to help you."

The ghost glared at me, then faded out of sight. My father blinked, as if a puff of wind had struck him in the eyes.

"She's gone, Mr. Tanleven!" said Chris. "Hurry!"

My dad returned his attention to the bedpost. Seconds later the knob turned in his hands.

We had no problem finding what was inside. The roll of papers hidden there extended past the top of the post; it must have been sticking right up into the hollow knob. Rolling the papers a little tighter, Dad pulled it out of the bedpost.

"Got it!" he said triumphantly. Then he looked guilty and stepped quickly away from the bed.

"Relax," I said. "She's still gone."

"But who knows when she'll be back," said Chris. "Come on, let's get out of here."

"Just my luck," my dad said as we left the room. "I finally meet a ghost, and other than a bit of a chill, I can't even tell it happened."

"Come on," said Byron impatiently. "I want to see what you've found." He led the way downstairs to the dining room. "We can spread the papers out here," he said, pointing to the big table.

"We'll have to do this carefully, so as not to damage the paper," my father said. He hesitated, then turned to Byron. "Actually, you should have the honor."

Byron reached forward, pulled his hand back, then reached out again and took the papers. For a minute I was afraid he might ask us to leave, so he could look at them in private. Even though he wouldn't have found the papers if it hadn't been for us, we had no real right to be here; if he wanted to throw us out, he could. But he didn't tell us to go. Instead, he laid the papers on the table, waited until we had all gathered around, and then slowly began to unroll them.

I was dying to know what they were. But part of me was enjoying the suspense: It was a little like unwrapping a present very slowly, to keep yourself waiting.

The papers kept wanting to curl back onto themselves.

"Hold down this end," Byron said to my father.

My dad leaned on the end of the paper and watched as Byron rolled it along the table to reveal what was inside. "Holy Moses!" he whispered.

The top sheet of paper held a Cornelius Fletcher drawing. I knew it was Fletcher's work, because by this time I could recognize his style. The drawing was one of his more pleasant pieces— a street scene in what looked like a little French village.

Byron leaned over to trace some of the lines with his fingertip. But he kept his hand about an inch above the paper, so that he wasn't actually touching it. "He was so good," he whispered, his voice filled with awe.

My father nodded.

Working slowly and carefully, they pulled apart the pages. There were a dozen drawings in all. We spread them around the table, holding them down at the corners with things from the kitchen—candlesticks and salt shakers, cream pitchers and spoon rests.

"You know what these are, don't you?" Byron asked after a minute.

"I've got a feeling," my father said.

I looked up. "Plans for his last painting?"

Byron nodded. "The Lost Masterpiece. What a tragedy he never finished it."

"Do we know that?" my father asked. "The rumor I always heard was that it had been painted but then disappeared somehow."

Byron shrugged. "Lost, stolen, or strayed— whatever happened to it, the world has lost a great piece of art."

I walked around the table, examining the pictures. I didn't stand too long in front of any of them—I was afraid they might start to draw me in, in the same way "Early Harvest" had done those other times. I was afraid of what I might see or feel if I let that happen.

I was afraid because even in the form of sketches, Cornelius Fletcher's art was almost too powerful to bear. It was filled with despair, but also with a fiery anger at a world that allowed the things he had experienced to happen.

"Look at this," whispered Chris. She was standing in front of a sketch of a hungry child with wide eyes. The work was savage and angry.

We moved on to the next sketch. Before I could examine it, the phone rang.

"Be back in a minute," Byron said. But it took even less time than that for him to return. He was pulling on his coat as he entered. "That was the hospital. Phoebe has taken a turn for the worse, and she's asking for me. Henry, I don't want to wait for a cab. Could you drive me over?"

"Of course," my father said.

"Do you want us to come?" I asked.

"I'd rather you took care of the sketches," said Byron. "I don't want to leave them lying out like this." He turned to my father and added, "That is, if you don't mind, Henry."

"No problem," said my father. "I'll be back here in a few minutes anyway. Come on, let's go."

They started for the front door. Chris and I followed them. My dad was halfway through the door when he turned back and said, "Look, don't do anything outlandish, will you?"

Normally I would have given him a wide-eyed look and played the "Who, *me*?" game. But this wasn't the time for that kind of thing, so I just shook my head.

He nodded, then turned and followed Byron out of the house.

"Poor old lady," Chris said. "I hope she's okay."

We started back down the hall. As we did, Chris grabbed my elbow. "Listen," she whispered.

Somewhere below us a thin, reedy voice was singing "'Over There.'"

CHAPTER TWENTY

Enough Rope to Hang Himself

"That's what I heard last night!" I whispered.

"Is it another ghost?"

"I don't know. Let's go see if we can find out."

Before I had time to worry about whether heading for the cellar would break my promise not to do anything outlandish, we had to scrap our plan, because something more urgent came up.

"Look," whispered Chris. "Up there!"

At the top of the stairs stood the ghost of Alida Fletcher. She stared at us for a moment, then gestured for us to come to her.

"Should we go?" asked Chris.

"Does *this* qualify as outlandish?" I asked.

Chris took a deep breath. "It would be outlandish if we went upstairs on our own. But since we're being invited . . ."

I shivered, remembering the feel of Alida's hands passing through me. "Do you think it's some sort of trap?"

Chris's eyes were locked on the top of the stairs. "No. You told her we wanted to help. I think she took you seriously."

"Me and my big mouth," I muttered as Chris started up the stairs—still holding me by the elbow.

The ghost waited until we had nearly reached her. Then she turned and began to climb the next flight of stairs, moving in that odd style ghosts have, something between walking and floating.

When we reached the third floor, we found another hallway, this one more narrow than the one below. The doors were all closed. Alida turned to the right, paused outside one of the doors, then passed through it. After a moment a translucent arm reached through the door and beckoned for us to follow.

Chris opened the door. On the other side was another stairway, clearly leading up to the attic.

"Just like with Captain Gray," I whispered, thinking of our adventure in the Quackadoodle Inn.

"Lots of secrets in old attics," Chris whispered back.

We followed the ghost up the stairway. The attic was dark. Since we hadn't brought a flashlight, our only light came from the faint glow of the ghost. She floated on, about ten feet ahead of us. Then she pointed at the floor and vanished, leaving us in the dark.

I made a squeak of fear. Chris tightened her grip on my elbow. "Don't worry," she whispered. "We know the way back. Let's see if we can figure out what she was pointing at."

"I don't think *see* is the right word."

"Well, then, we'll *feel* it," said Chris crossly. "Come on."

We inched our way forward. When we were close to the spot where the ghost had disappeared, I stepped on something that rolled beneath my feet.

"Snake!" I cried, jumping back in terror. I fell and lay in the darkness, gasping for breath.

"Nine, don't do that to me!" cried Chris. Then she started to laugh.

"What's so funny?" I snapped.

"Here's your snake. It's a pile of rope."

I laughed a little, too. Then I stopped. "Chris, are you thinking what I'm thinking?"

"Jimmy."

" 'I hung him,' " I whispered, repeating Jimmy's words.

I shivered and looked around, half expecting the ghost of Cornelius Fletcher to come floating out of the darkness.

"Come on," I said. "Let's get out of here."

It took us a moment to find each other in the dark. While I was groping around, I had the sense that we were surrounded by rope. The coils seemed to be everywhere. For a moment I was tangled in them.

"Here!" Chris grabbed my hand. "Let's go."

Clinging to each other, we made our way back to the attic stairs. We continued to hold on to each other, even after we had made it to the third-floor hall, where there was enough light from below so we could at least make out shapes and doors.

On the next floor we considered taking a peek in the tower room, to see if the ghost was there. "Forget it," said Chris. "If she wants anything else, she can come and get us."

I nodded, and we continued to the ground floor. I hoped my father would be back soon. I had had enough for one night.

"The sketches!" Chris exclaimed, "We're supposed to put away the sketches."

She headed toward the dining room. I started to follow, then stopped. The door to the parlor was open, and the little light that was mounted above "Early Harvest" was on. I shuddered. I didn't particularly want to look at the picture again.

On the other hand, I was sure it held at least part of the key to what was going on in this house.

Before I knew what I was doing, I found myself standing in the parlor, staring at the picture.

Soon I could feel the change begin. I tried to break away, but before I could move, the past reached out and took me in. Once more I heard guns booming in the distance, smelled the smoke and the blood. Nearby, men were screaming. We were in retreat.

I ran, too. But my flight to safety came to a stop when a hand reached out and grabbed my leg. Spinning around, I saw a man staring up at me. He was young, hardly more than a boy, really. His face was smeared with blood.

"Help me," he gasped. "Cornelius, for the love of God, *help me!*"

I reached down and pulled him into my arms.

I was startled to realize that my arms were much stronger than they should have been. It wasn't until later that I understood I was reliving the events that had brought Cornelius Fletcher to paint "Early Harvest." When I spoke, I repeated the words he had spoken; when I moved, I was making the movements he had been remembering as he painted.

Trapped in someone else's memory, I carried the wounded man away from the battle. My heart was pounding with the fear of death, and I wanted to drop him so that I could save myself. Shells continued to explode around us, but still I held on to the wounded man.

I was not being heroic—I was reliving *Cornelius's* act of heroism. I was also reliving his feelings. So I knew just how scared he had been when this happened—as scared as I was now. For the first time I really understood that bravery doesn't

mean not being afraid; it means doing what has to
be done even if you're terrified.

The force of an exploding shell threw me to
my knees. With great effort I stood up again. The
noise around us was deafening. I wanted to get
away, but I couldn't, couldn't go fast enough, far
enough, because death was everywhere.

Suddenly the young man I carried cried out. I
looked again at his horrible wound, and I knew
that if I didn't stop to bind it, stop here, now, in the
middle of the shelling, the explosions, the fire,
he would be dead by the time I got him back to the
medics.

I knelt—which means that Cornelius knelt—
and used my knife to shred my shirt, which I
bound around his wounds.

I was glad it was really Cornelius binding the
wound, and not me, because I don't think I could
have managed without fainting. I won't describe
what it looked like; even now remembering the
sight makes my stomach start to churn.

At last I was on my feet again, heading for the
trench. I passed other dying men. Many of them. I
began to weep, in sorrow, and in rage, because
there were so many young men dying here, and I
could save only one—carry only the one I already
held out of the bloodbath surrounding us.

The tears belonged to Cornelius. But they
were my tears, too.

I staggered on. Finally the trench was in sight.

I cried out for help. Two men scrambled forward. As they did, a shell exploded behind me.

I felt my legs twist and tear, and I screamed in agony.

Then everything went black.

CHAPTER TWENTY-ONE

Hanging Around

When I opened my eyes, Chris was standing over me. She looked worried. After a moment I realized that my head was being held off the floor. It wasn't until I heard my father say, "Nine! Nine, are you all right?" that I realized he was kneeling behind me, holding my head in his lap.

I blinked. "I think so," I said at last.

"What happened?" asked Chris.

"I got caught in the painting again. Only this time I saw the whole thing. It's about what happened to Cornelius the day he was wounded." I paused. "Remember what Marcus told us—that Cornelius saved Hiram Potter's son?"

Chris nodded, looking puzzled.

"What he didn't say—didn't know, I imagine—was that it was taking the time to save Potter's son that got Cornelius crippled."

"No wonder Potter felt so guilty when he learned the whole story!" said Chris, her eyes wide.

"Come on," my father said, lifting my shoulders. "We're getting out of here."

"What about Phoebe?" I asked as he helped me to my feet. "How is she doing?"

"We won't know for a while," he said, his face troubled. "She's on the edge. The doctor says if she makes it through the night, she has a fair chance of recovering. Unfortunately, that seems to be a pretty big if. Anyway, *you're* the one I'm worried about right now."

"I'm fine," I said. "Just a little shaken up."

As it turned out, I was more than a "little" shaken up. The events I had seen while in the spell of Cornelius Fletcher's painting seemed to haunt me as the days went past. Every night my dreams replayed his fight to save Hiram Potter's son. Every night I woke up screaming.

The painting haunted me. The little girl in the bed haunted me. The voice in the cellar and the ghost outside haunted me. A neat trick, since all of them were at the Watson house, which I didn't go anywhere near for the next several days. But they seemed to circle constantly in my head, demanding that I solve their mystery, put the picture together, untie the knot that kept the two—or was it three?—ghosts tied to the house.

On the fourth day my father put his foot down. "Look, Nine, I know you've got a lot on your mind. But what goes on at Phoebe Watson's house is really not your business. School is, and I expect you to start concentrating on your work and getting things done on time again."

This speech was brought on by a note that came home from my teacher.

I couldn't really blame my dad. I had always been a pretty good student. (Not great, but not bad, either.) But I had become so obsessed with Phoebe's home that I had really let things slide. I wanted to go talk to Phoebe, but she was in intensive care and couldn't have any visitors besides Byron.

We called every day to ask about her. She was getting better—slowly, but more surely than the doctor had expected.

Dad had several long talks with Mona Curtis. I wasn't sure, but I think they were about me. At least, I know he told her what had happened, because Mona asked me about it once when she was talking to me.

"Hard to tell what's going on, exactly," she said after I had told her the story in my own words. "My guess is that when Fletcher was painting 'Early Harvest,' he poured all his memories of that event into the work. The sensitivity you've been developing because of your experience with ghosts allowed you to tap into that energy and relive the experience."

As if experiencing the painting wasn't enough to cope with, I had to deal with the fact that Chris was upset because she hadn't been there with me.

"I can't believe you did that!" she said.

"It wasn't like I meant to," I replied. "It was almost as though the picture was calling to me. I think that I was more linked into it because I had already seen it a second time, the night I went over there during the storm."

Chris understood that. But it didn't make her any happier about having missed out. I kept trying to tell her it wasn't the kind of thing she necessarily wanted to experience for herself.

Even though she was slightly miffed, the two of us spent hours on the phone, trying to straighten out the tangle of information we had gathered.

"All right, the ghost in the bed is Phoebe's little sister," said Chris one afternoon as we were sorting through what we knew for the umpteenth time.

"Big sister."

"How can she be Phoebe's big sister? She's a little kid."

"Yeah, but she was born *before* Phoebe, so that makes her the big sister."

"Let's just say she's Phoebe's sister and leave it at that," Chris said impatiently. "Now the guy outside is her father. What I don't get is this: If the kid is hanging around because she's waiting for her father to come get her, why doesn't he just come inside and settle things?"

"Mona thinks he can't," I replied. "He feels guilty because his daughter died while he was outside, trying to get in. Now he's reliving that tragedy—still trying to come through for her. But he's trapped outside by his own failure."

"I don't know," said Chris. "I'd buy that if he had actually *died* out there. But he made it back inside the next morning and lived there for a while. Doesn't sound to me like the way a ghost would operate."

What she said made some sense. But I wasn't sure if she really believed it or if she was just resisting the other idea because it came from Mona.

"The other question is, who's in the cellar?"

"That reminds me," said Chris, "I found out about the song."

"What song?"

"The one we heard coming from the cellar. I asked my father."

That made sense. Chris's father has a real thing about musical theater, so he knows lots about old songs, even ones that haven't come from Broadway shows.

"It was kind of our unofficial anthem for World War One," she continued. "All about how the bright and brave Americans were going to go 'Over There' and save Europe. He's got a record of it—I'll play it the next time you're over."

"That may be Saturday," I said. "Norma called last night and asked if I wanted to work."

I had been a little hesitant about saying yes. I had found out Phoebe was coming home on Wednesday, and what I really wanted to do that weekend was go back over to her house and snoop. But under the circumstances it seemed a little tacky. Besides, working at Norma's *would* give me a chance to spend the night with Chris. So I had said yes.

Norma, of course, wanted me to fill her in on everything that had happened—even though she had already heard most of it from my father. "That's not the same as hearing it from you," she said. "Your dad doesn't really like to talk about it. I think it embarrasses him a little. You're much better on details."

After a while I began to wonder whether Norma had brought me to the shop to work or to answer questions about our adventures.

It turned out that Chris's parents had plans for that evening. So instead of my staying at her place, she was going to ride home with Norma and me, to stay at my house.

At the end of the day the two of us were waiting outside while Norma did some last-minute paperwork. We were sitting on the stone wall that ran in front of the shop, talking about Phoebe Watson, when a voice called to us from the bushes.

"Something terrible, something wonderful, haven't found it yet."

I jumped off the wall and ran over to the hedge. "Jimmy! Jimmy, what's up there at Phoebe's House?"

"Can't tell!" said Jimmy. He sounded offended, as if I had asked him to do something wicked.

"What about the ropes?" I asked, backing away a bit. "What do you know about the ropes?"

"Can't hang someone without ropes."

"Did you really hang Cornelius Fletcher?" Chris asked sharply. She had come over to stand beside me.

Jimmy's eyes went wide. "Had to! Poor man couldn't do it himself. I hung him every day."

Just then Norma came out of the shop. At the sound of the door opening Jimmy ducked into the bushes.

"You two ready to stop chasing squirrels and go home?" called Norma.

"We're not after squirrels," Chris replied. "We're talking to a nut."

"Maybe," I said softly. "And maybe not."

"He's nuts," Chris said. "You can only hang a guy once; after that he's dead!"

I wasn't so sure about that. I was starting to get an idea. Everything clicked into place as we drove past Seven Rays.

Well, not everything. But I knew why Jimmy had hung Cornelius Fletcher.

And I knew where the Lost Masterpiece was.

CHAPTER TWENTY-TWO

On the Edge

"You're as crazy as Jimmy," said Chris when I told her my theory.

"Fine," I said. "You don't have to believe me. I'll test it on my own."

"How?"

She had me there. Phoebe Watson's house wasn't a public place, like the Grand Theater or the Quackadoodle Inn. In those places Chris and I had been fairly free to wander around. But I had no excuse for snooping through Phoebe's house—at least, not the kind of excuse anyone other than Chris or I would go for.

"We could just ask," she said at last.

Notice that even though she thought I was nuts, she was willing to help me test my theory.

I thought about what she had said for a minute, then began to laugh. We had gotten so used to doing things in secret that it hadn't occurred to me that we could simply *ask* Byron or Phoebe to let us test my theory.

"Let's go call them," I said.

As it turned out, we didn't need to. The phone was ringing when we left my room. My father got to it first. He listened for a moment, then said, "Hold on. I'll check." Putting his hand over the mouthpiece, he turned to us and said, "It's Byron. He wants to know if you two can spend the night."

I must have looked astonished because my father started to laugh. "Byron wants you to baby-sit. He's been tied to the house for the last few days, and he's starting to get cabin fever. He'd like to go out with some friends, but he doesn't feel he can leave Phoebe alone. She sleeps a lot of the time, but he wants someone there to bring her medicine and water, talk to her if she's awake, things like that."

I looked at Chris and smiled. When the gods put a gift like this in your lap, you don't question it.

"We'd be glad to help," I said.

"I figured as much," replied Dad. "On the other hand, I'm not so sure I want you over there."

"Oh, Dad, the ghosts are no problem. They never really tried to harm us—and you know yourself that they can't hurt you if they hit you."

"You can cause people damage without hitting them," he said. "For example, you could slam a shutter on them."

I wondered if Mona had given him that line or if he had come up with it on his own.

"Anyway," he continued, "it's not the ghosts I'm worried about. It's 'Early Harvest.' I'm not willing to let you go unless you promise you'll stay away from that picture."

I hate having to stay away from anything. On the other hand, I figured I had already learned all I was going to learn from "Early Harvest." So I promised.

"You, too," he said to Chris.

"Won't be a problem," Chris said casually.

My father looked at her. "How dumb do you think I am?" he said. "Promise."

Chris sighed. "I promise, Mr. Tanleven."

Dad nodded and turned back to the phone. "You're on, Byron." He listened for a moment, then said, "No, don't bother to send a cab. I'll bring them over. I need to pick up some groceries anyway."

He hung up and told us to pack our overnight bags. Chris hadn't *un*packed hers yet, so she was all set.

As soon as we were finished with supper, the three of us piled into the Golden Chariot and took off for Phoebe Watson's house and our appointment with destiny.

(When my dad first read that sentence, he said he thought I was being overly dramatic. But when I reminded him of everything that had happened that night, he decided I was right to use it.)

Byron greeted us at the door. "I'm so glad you two could do this," he said. "I love Phoebe, I really do. But I think one more night alone with her in this house and I would have lost my mind."

"Another mad artist," I said without thinking.

Chris and my dad gave me a look that said, "Well, now that your foot is in your mouth, how does it taste?"

Byron, being a gentleman, changed the subject. "Phoebe is resting in the dining room."

"Kind of a strange place to rest," said Chris.

"We decided it would be easier on everyone if she could stay on the ground floor. Some friend of hers—Carla Bond, I think—loaned us some money to rent a hospital bed."

"Does Phoebe know we're going to be here?" I asked.

Byron nodded. "She's a little embarrassed about it—feels that she's being a lot of bother. But she's glad to have you here. She really likes the two of you."

"Adorable, aren't they?" my father said.

I had a feeling he didn't mean for us to take him seriously.

Dad and Byron talked for a few more minutes, then Dad told us to be careful, reminded me of my promise, gave each of us a hug, and took off.

After my father left, Byron showed us where Phoebe's heart medicine was. Then he took us to

the kitchen. He was telling us about the buzzers
he had rigged up for her to call him when a horn
began to honk outside.

"That's my ride. Remember, whenever you get
tired, you can go to bed in Phoebe's room. I'll see
you later!"

We went to the door with him. Then we returned to the kitchen and made ourselves a little
snack. I tried to do some homework. I couldn't concentrate. The only thing I was really interested in
doing right now was testing my theory. But I had
to get someone's permission first.

I figured we had two chances. If Phoebe woke
up and was feeling well, we could ask her. Or we
could wait until Byron got back and ask him—although I thought I might pop if I had to wait that
long.

Fortunately—or maybe unfortunately—
things moved faster than that.

We were just debating whether or not to have
some more ice cream when a buzzer sounded.
Phoebe was awake and needed something.

We headed for the dining room. I was a little
surprised when we entered. I knew it had been
made into a sickroom. But it was still strange to
see the big table pushed against the wall and a
metal bed in the middle of the room.

Phoebe looked smaller than I remembered, as
if she had shrunk while she was ill. Her pale skin

seemed almost translucent. Yet the smile on her face was bright and strong.

"It is so good to see the two of you again," she said, holding her hands out to us.

"Good to see you, too, Phoebe," I said, trying to sound cheerful.

"Pshaw," she said, which surprised me, since I always thought that that was a sound people only made in books. "What would the two of you want to see an old prune like me for? But it was awfully nice of you to come over and give Byron a break. The poor boy needs a little time off. Now, help me up, would you?"

A wheelchair stood beside the bed. Following Phoebe's directions, we cranked up the back of the bed and maneuvered her around so she could slip into the wheelchair without much trouble. We covered her legs with a thick afghan.

"Let's go sit in the parlor," she said. "We can chat, maybe even play a little game."

That was fine with me; I wanted to be in the parlor—though Chris and I were going to have to be careful to keep from looking at "Early Harvest."

We got Phoebe settled. Then I made some tea.

"Well, isn't this cozy," said Phoebe as I rolled in the tea cart. She adjusted the afghan we had spread over her lap and said, "Now we can have a good old-fashioned chat."

"Can we talk about the old days?" I asked.

"Of course," she said, with a little smile. "Truth to tell, I don't think I do a very good job talking about anything else. The world is changing too fast for me to keep up with it. I'm not complaining, mind you. It's been a pretty good life, all in all, even if things were sort of rocky at the beginning." She sighed. "Actually, the only regret I have is that I won't be able to pass the house on to Byron. Well that, and never finding Poppa's last picture. Oh, girls, that would have done him such honor. It would have put him where he belongs— not in the footnotes, but right in the center of the art history of his time."

This was the opening I had been waiting for. My stomach felt tight. "I think I know where the picture is," I said softly.

For a moment no one spoke. The silence in the room felt heavy.

"Nine," said Phoebe slowly. "Please don't tease me about this."

"I'm not teasing. I have a theory."

"She's figured out things like this before," said Chris.

I looked at her in surprise. Chris shrugged. I felt good; it was nice to have her stick up for me.

Phoebe looked at me carefully. "Are you quite certain?" Her fingers picked at the edge of her afghan.

Now I felt nervous. "I'm not *certain*. It's only a theory. But if we don't try, we'll never find out."

Phoebe was quiet for a little while. "I have to call Carla," she said at last.

I gave her a questioning look.

"Carla has spent the last thirty years studying Poppa's work. If you're correct, I want her to be here when his masterpiece is unveiled. She's earned that right—or at least the right to have a chance." With a bit of a twinkle in her eye she added, "But if Carla isn't home, I won't make you wait until she gets back."

Carla Bond *was* home. I would have been impatient waiting for her, but I remembered the night I begged my father to drive over and get Chris before we opened the strongbox from the gazebo. So I understood how Phoebe felt.

To my relief, Ms. Bond lived less than a mile away. Even so, it seemed like hours before we heard the doorbell. When it rang, I jumped up and shouted, which made Chris laugh. "Calm down," she said. "You can't make your theory right by worrying about it."

We started for the door. But Ms. Bond didn't wait for anyone; she just opened the door and walked in.

"It's me!" she called from the hallway. "Thank you so much for thinking of me," she continued as she came into the parlor. "I would have been crushed if I had missed this." She crossed the room to give Phoebe a kiss on the cheek. "You know how I have dreamed of this."

She took a seat, looked at me, and said, "Well, let's hear your little theory."

Suddenly I was frightened. Ms. Bond had been studying Cornelius Fletcher for years. If my idea was right, why hadn't she figured it out on her own? I had to be wrong.

I don't know what I was afraid of; it wasn't as if Ms. Bond would hit me if I was wrong, or anything like that. I just didn't want to feel her scorn. I had a sense that she was good at scorn, could crank out the kind that made you want to shrink down and hide behind a rock.

I explained my theory.

Ms. Bond closed her eyes for a moment. A look of profound sorrow crossed her face.

"Oh, my dear girl," she said. "I was so hoping that you would be wrong."

"Why in the world would you want her to be wrong?" asked Chris.

"Because then I could have let the three of you live," replied Ms. Bond. Reaching into her purse, she pulled out a small gun. Pointing it directly at my head, she said, "As it turns out, I can't let any of you leave this room alive."

CHAPTER TWENTY-THREE

Off the Wall

"Carla!" gasped Phoebe, clutching at her heart. "Carla, what are you doing?"

"Protecting my investment."

"What do you mean?"

"Oh, think, Phoebe," she snapped. "I've been trying to buy this house from you for over ten years now. Didn't you ever wonder why I've been so interested in it?"

"Because you know where the picture is," I said softly.

Ms. Bond turned to me. "That's right, Nine. But then, you have a habit of being right when you'd be better off being wrong. You see, I can't afford to let that picture come to light just yet. It's my retirement fund, dear—the total investment of my life's work."

"What do you mean?" Chris asked.

"Figure it out for yourself," snapped Ms. Bond. She took a little breath, then added, "This isn't the end of some book, where the villain kindly explains all his motives so you can know what's going on. So just think about it, while I figure out what I'm going to do with the three of you. As the witch said in *The Wizard of Oz,* 'These things must be done delicately.' I have to make sure no one can trace any of this back to me."

"Carla," said Phoebe, "let the girls go."

"The girls, my dear, are the problem. *Your* death is easy enough to explain; you'll probably be gone from a heart attack by the time I'm finished with these two anyway. What I need is something to explain *their* deaths." She paused, then said, "I think a break-in is the ticket."

I was annoyed. The last guy who tried to kill Chris and me wanted to make it look like a suicide. Now Ms. Bond was going to blame some non-existent burglar. I wanted to tell her to grow up and take responsibility for her own actions. But I didn't say that. Instead, I asked, "Is this place really worth the risk of killing us?"

"Shut up," she explained.

Since Ms. Bond wasn't going to help, I had to figure things out on my own. It wasn't hard. Given what my dad had told me about Cornelius Fletcher's Lost Masterpiece, combined with what I had figured out on my own, I could guess what Phoebe's house was worth. If Carla could buy it at a regular price—probably under a hundred thousand—the difference would be almost pure profit.

Which meant my big mouth was about to cost Carla a few *million* dollars.

I could see why she was upset with me. Under the circumstances I would have been unhappy, too.

The difference is, I wouldn't have been willing to kill someone to keep it from happening.

But in a world where people are getting killed for the sake of their wallets, I suppose it shouldn't have been surprising that someone was willing to bump me off for a few million.

If I sound calm now, believe me, I was sweating bullets at the time. Nice cliché; if I could have sweated a gun to go with them, I would have been all set.

When Ms. Bond spoke again, her voice was as cold as February; her words carried that coldness into my blood.

"Maybe I don't need to worry about delicacy," she said. "Perhaps crude will do just fine under the circumstances. On your faces, girls—and hands behind your backs."

My heart was pounding. I looked at Chris. Her eyes were wide—and hopeless. I knew what she was feeling. It looked as though this time we had finally gotten in over our heads.

"On your faces!" repeated Ms. Bond.

I thought about resisting. No point—the woman would only blow me away that much sooner. Or maybe there *was* a point. Maybe by resisting, I could give Chris a chance to escape. On the other hand, maybe something else would happen. Maybe Byron would realize he had forgotten something and come walking through the front door. Maybe my father would decide he was lonely and come over for a chat.

Or maybe nothing would happen, and I would have to do it myself. If so, I decided to wait as long as I could; I didn't want to get myself blown away mere seconds before rescue arrived.

"All right, here's the picture," Ms. Bond said. At first I thought she meant the Lost Masterpiece. Then I realized she was talking to herself, outlining her plan. "Burglar breaks in, finds girls in living room, kills them so they can't identify him. Old woman hears commotion, too much for her weak heart, bang—she's gone, too. Probably better get Phoebe back into her bed before I finish her off."

"Carla!" said Phoebe desperately.

"You're not going to turn me away, Phoebe. I've been waiting decades for this, and I'll not be stopped now."

She walked over and stood behind me. Suddenly I felt cold metal against the back of my neck. "Now how would a burglar do this?" she muttered to herself. "From close up—or farther back?"

"My God, Carla, listen to yourself," pleaded Phoebe. "This isn't you. You're a woman of culture. Stop before it's too late."

"It's been too late for over sixty years."

If things had gone on much longer, I probably would have died of fright before Ms. Bond had a chance to shoot me. But suddenly a new voice spoke.

"Put down the gun, little sister."

"Jimmy!" I cried in astonishment. "What are you doing here?"

"Quiet!" snapped Ms. Bond. "Both of you. Jimmy, get out of here. Now!"

"I can't do that," said Jimmy, stepping forward. "I can't let you hurt Cornelius's daughter."

"He killed our father!" Ms. Bond screamed. "What do you care anyway, you traitor?"

"Our father killed himself," Jimmy said. "And that should have been the end of it. But it wasn't, was it? Oh, no, it wasn't anywhere near the end."

Chris inched a little closer to me. "What the heck is going on here?" she whispered.

"I don't have the slightest idea," I hissed back.

Ms. Bond was facing Jimmy now, pointing the gun at the crazy old man I used to feed, the coot who had come to our rescue.

He had no real weapon to fend her off, only a weathered two-by-four that he carried between his gnarled hands. He was so old and frail, I didn't know if that would do him—or us—any good.

"Jimmy, I swear I'll shoot you, too," Ms. Bond said. Her voice was trembling, but she raised her gun and pointed it directly at his chest.

I gathered myself. I could feel Chris doing the same thing. We might be able to rush Ms. Bond while she was concentrating on Jimmy. But we hesitated. If we attacked, she might just fire wildly. She could hit any one of us before we managed to get the gun out of her hands.

"Jimmy, you can leave here alive," continued Ms. Bond. Her voice was low, pleading. "I don't need to kill you. Even if you did tell what happened here, no one would believe it. You can't hurt me. So turn around and go. Go, damn you!"

"I can't. This is my home. I have to protect it."

"What do you mean?" asked Ms. Bond. She was almost shrieking. "This isn't your home."

"Yes, it is," whispered Phoebe. "He lives in the basement when it gets too cold or wet outside. He's been there off and on for years."

Boing! That explained the singing. Cross off the three-ghost theory; it was two ghosts and a nut.

"Couldn't you even give him a decent room?" Ms. Bond screamed, swinging the gun toward Phoebe.

"I offered," said Phoebe. "I offered, but . . ." Her voice trailed off, and she clutched at her chest.

"Ms. Bond," I said desperately, "she has to have her medicine. Let me get her medicine."

"Shut up!"

"Carla . . ." gasped Phoebe. Her voice sounded raspy and strangled. She began to tip forward.

Jimmy lunged at his sister. She fired the pistol. Jimmy fell, clutching his arm.

"Cornelius!" he cried. *"Cornelius, for the love of God, help me!"*

I shivered. They were the same words, the same cry, the same *voice* I had heard the night "Early Harvest" drew me in and told me its entire story. It was as if Jimmy's younger self were calling across time.

Cornelius Fletcher heard it, too. Not the daughter he had lost, but the man he had saved. Not his failure calling, but his success. This he could do. Suddenly the air of the room was filled with a great cry of rage as the ghost of Cornelius Fletcher appeared inside his home for the first time since his death. His angry spirit turned in a slow circle, taking in the scene. When he saw Phoebe, bent forward in her chair, clutching her heart, his mad eyes began to blaze.

Ms. Bond's face was white; her whole body shook with astonishment. "Go away!" she screamed. "You're not real. Go away!"

Cornelius didn't move.

She fired her pistol, once, twice, three times.

Cornelius moved toward her, his face more terrible than anything I had ever seen. Ms. Bond spun toward me, then pointed the gun at me. "Go away, or the girl dies!"

Before I had time to faint, a terrible shredding sound ripped through the room. Turning my

head, I gasped as I saw a long strip of paper peel
away from the wall. Faster than I can write this
sentence, the paper flew across the room and
wrapped itself around Carla Bond.

I could see bright colors where the paper had
been torn from the wall.

I whooped in jubilation. I had been right!

Rip! Rip! Rip!

You could feel the power swirling around Cornelius as he used his ghostly abilities to strip the
aging paper from the walls and bind it around
Carla.

When he was finally done and silence descended on the room, we found ourselves staring
in awe at something more terrible, more wonderful than I had ever imagined.

CHAPTER TWENTY-FOUR

Over There

An hour later my father stood in the center of Phoebe Watson's parlor, turning and turning as he studied the Lost Masterpiece.

"It's magnificent," he whispered, his eyes filling with tears. "So terrible, but so beautiful."

I knew what he meant.

Cornelius Fletcher's last painting was a vast mural, a picture that started in the parlor, then stretched to the hall, and then to the dining room, and on, until it covered every wall on the first floor of the house. It was a painting nearly unbearable in its sense of pain and betrayal and lost love.

Now that painting surrounded a small mob of people. My dad was there, along with Norma Bliss. (It turned out that the two of them had had a date that night, a fact concerning which I was less than amused.) We also had half a dozen cops, a doctor, Jimmy, and Carla Bond. Byron was there, too—the cops had managed to locate the bar where he had gone with his friends. Stephen Bassett was also present, acting as Ms. Bond's lawyer.

The only one missing was Phoebe. She had taken her last breath during the battle between her father and Ms. Bond.

An ambulance had come, and medics carried her away. But it was too late. I knew that for a certainty. Now I only wanted to go home and think. But first we had to answer questions from the police and almost everyone else in the room. That wasn't all that bad—at least we got to hear some answers from Jimmy and Ms. Bond, too.

By the time the session was over, the picture was pretty well filled in.

"The picture was pretty well filled in"—a good phrase to use here, all things considered.

That was one of the first questions *I* had to answer, of course—"How did you know where the picture was?"

"To tell you the truth, it was more hunch than knowledge," I said. "Mostly it came from the way little things began to fit together. When enough of them connected, everything seemed to make sense."

"What kinds of little things?" asked my father.

"Actually, you gave me the first clue, even though I didn't realize it at the time."

He looked blank.

"Stripping wallpaper," I said, and laughed. "You put the idea in my head that wallpaper covered up what had been on the wall before. Then there was the mural being painted at Seven Rays; it reminded me that artists don't have to paint on canvas, that they can use a whole wall if they want. Then there were the ropes we found in the attic. Too many ropes for a simple hanging."

"He couldn't have done it without me," muttered Jimmy, staring at the painting. He was on the sofa. A blanket covered his dirty, ragged clothes, and he was sipping coffee from a cup Norma had brought him. "I hung him every day, so he could work."

As I looked around the room, I could imagine the scene. Cornelius Fletcher, his legs gone, half mad—or maybe completely crazy—consumed with the passion for creating his final masterpiece. But he couldn't do it on his own. So he had his assistant, Jimmy, the boy he had saved in the war, help him. Jimmy rigged pulleys and ropes and scaffolds all around the house, and came in every day to strap Cornelius into a harness and pull the legless artist into the air, so he could hang there and work.

I looked at the wall in front of me, with its terrible images of battle, images that overwhelmed even "Early Harvest." I could imagine Cornelius hanging from a harness in front of it, desperately painting, feverish with inspiration.

"Father hated you for helping him," Ms. Bond said bitterly.

"Father didn't know Cornelius had saved my life," wheezed Jimmy. "He wouldn't listen until it was too late."

The police kept trying to ask Ms. Bond questions. At first Mr. Bassett wouldn't let her answer. But finally she snapped, "It doesn't matter now. They might as well know."

Shrugging, Mr. Bassett sat back. I had the sense that he felt he had done his duty by counseling Ms. Bond to silence. Since he was her lawyer, he had to try to protect her. But that didn't mean he had to like what she had tried to do. If she wanted to brush him off now, that was fine with Mr. Bassett.

"After Alida died, Cornelius completely lost touch with reality," said Carla. "It wasn't long before his wife, Amanda, fled to live with her sister. Four years later, when Cornelius became ill, she returned to care for him, bringing Phoebe with her.

"But Cornelius was dead before she arrived.

"Phoebe was three at the time. Her mother brought her into the house, and when the little girl saw the mural and the ropes still hanging in front of it, she began to scream. Amanda swept Phoebe out of the house and had the entire first floor papered over before she would bring the child back."

"I did that for her," interrupted Jimmy, tears streaming down his face. "It nearly killed me, but I covered his picture, and I promised I would never tell. It scared the little girl too much. Never did tell, either," he added, sounding proud.

"Phoebe saw the painting only once," continued Ms. Bond. "But the impact was so extreme that the memory never left her. She pushed the experience to the back of her mind, where it haunted her dreams. She used to have nightmares about ropes and pulleys, though she didn't know why. She told me about them, about how she would wake up in the middle of the night, trembling and covered with sweat, screaming, 'The ropes, the ropes!' She was sure there was more. Only she could never remember what the rest of the nightmare was about.

"But I knew. Even though I had never seen it myself, I figured it out from her dreams. And I vowed I would own it someday—payment for what happened to my family."

"Your family?" Norma asked. "Seems to me it was Phoebe's family that suffered."

Ms. Bond snorted. "My father was a suicide. My brother became a bum, and my mother lived on the dole while she tried to raise me singlehandedly through the Depression. Is that enough to qualify for family problems?

"But I knew where there was something worth enough money to make up for all of it. Even

though Jimmy never told, I figured it out. And all
I had to do was buy this house. Only the witch
wouldn't sell. She clung to this old place that was
ten times as big as she needed, clung to it in the
memory of her sainted father."

Ms. Bond's eyes were blazing. She spat on the
floor.

I thought about making some crack about civ-
ilized behavior, but realized that this was not the
time. Sure, she had been going to blow me away a
little while ago. But now I realized that I was
watching a woman have a nervous breakdown
right before my very eyes. It was, perhaps, the
most frightening thing that happened in that
long, frightening month.

"I went to school—*worked* my way through,
without help from anyone. Made a name inter-
preting the work of Cornelius Fletcher. And kept
looking for my chance to get the house. I had it all
set finally. Phoebe was broke, ready to sell. If she
died, the house would go to Byron, and he had
agreed to sell it to me."

Byron blushed. "Carla loaned me money to
pay the hospital bills in return for a promise to
sell," he said. What a generous man; he had
agreed to give up any inheritance he might have
in order to help Phoebe.

"It would have been two triumphs in one
stroke," Ms. Bond continued. "Once I unveiled
Fletcher's last work, I would have been able to

write my own ticket in the art world. And the money! Oh, at last I would have the money I needed to live the way I deserved. A fortune! And it was all so close, until this brat opened her mouth."

That's me—Big-Mouth of the Century.

But I didn't regret it. Even if things hadn't worked out entirely the way I would have liked, given what had happened in Phoebe's parlor before the police arrived, I couldn't feel entirely bad about them either.

Once Cornelius appeared, things had moved fast for a while. Ms. Bond, wrapped in at least a dozen layers of wallpaper, was out of the picture for the time being. But the action continued when Alida Fletcher appeared at the top of the stairs calling, "Daddy? Oh, Daddy, is that you?"

I had felt my eyes fill with tears as her tiny figure came drifting down the stairs.

"Oh, Daddy!" she whispered joyously.

A cry seemed to split the room, the sound of a great heart breaking, as Cornelius Fletcher stepped forward and held out his arms to the daughter he had been unable to save, the child who had waited over sixty years for him to keep his promise to come back for her.

"Poppa!" cried another voice—an old, weak voice.

I turned and saw Phoebe start up from her wheelchair. "Poppa!" she cried again.

Then she fell forward and lay still on the floor. For a moment no one moved. Utter silence, deep and mysterious, filled the room.

Then a translucent form rose from Phoebe's still body. *"Poppa,"* she whispered again.

I blinked. Phoebe's ghost was a little girl. Then suddenly it was a grown woman, then an old lady, and just as suddenly a little girl again.

As the spirit of Phoebe Fletcher Watson floated across the parlor it continued to shift back and forth between all the people she had been through her long lifetime. But it was as a little girl that she reached out and took her father's hand. He drew her to him, and the three of them stood together—the mad artist, the child he had failed, and the child he had never met.

I trembled with emotion. I don't know what to call it: It wasn't sorrow or joy. It was simply more feeling than I could possibly hold.

Chris reached out and took my hand. I squeezed hard and hung on.

"Cornelius!" cried Jimmy Potter, his voice for an instant young with joy and recognition. "Cornelius!"

Cornelius Fletcher turned and nodded solemnly to the man he had twice saved, the man whose father had crippled him and cost him his child.

Then he took each daughter by the hand. Together they circled the room, slowly examining the great painting.

As I followed them with my eyes, they came to a place beside the door, and I realized that I had been wrong; Cornelius Fletcher's painting was *not* complete.

I remembered the despairing words of his final letter: "I cannot finish it."

Here was the spot that had defeated him. This was the place where the battle broke, where the death and the pain disappeared. It was the place where the artist had stopped, because he had reached the scene he could not paint—the scene of ending, of peace, of satisfaction.

But now, at last, he was ready. Putting both hands forward, Cornelius Fletcher laid them on the wall.

A sob tore from him, a final cry of surrender, and completion and acceptance. The colors of solace flowed beneath his fingers, and the empty place on the wall was soon filled with the image of a peaceful woodland under a clear blue sky—the place of peace beyond the battle.

The Lost Masterpiece was finally finished.

From somewhere past Cornelius's sky I heard the sound of singing—voices soft at first, growing louder and more clear as they repeated the anthem of World War I, the promise we had made to a dying continent. Only now the words had a different meaning, a different promise.

"'Over there,'" sang the voices. "'Over there . . .'"

Taking his daughters' hands again, Cornelius Fletcher stepped toward his painting.

Wiping away my tears, I watched with joy as he led Phoebe and Alida to the place of peace he had finally been able to create.

As the artist and his daughters stepped into the painting, the colors began to fade. Within moments the vision of peace had disappeared, gone with Cornelius and his daughters.

But I know it's there, waiting beyond the battle.

The place of peace.

Over there.

ABOUT THE AUTHOR

Bruce Coville is the author of more than eighty books for young readers, including *My Teacher Is an Alien, Into the Land of the Unicorns,* and, of course, the Nina Tanleven ghost stories. He has also written short stories, magazine articles, poems, a science fiction novel for adults, and three musical plays for young audiences. His love of theater helped prompt him to write the first Nina Tanleven book, *The Ghost in the Third Row.*

Born and raised in upstate New York, Bruce Coville worked as a teacher, a toy maker, a magazine editor, and a gravedigger before becoming a full-time writer. Much in demand as a speaker, he spends considerable time traveling around the country to make presentations at schools, libraries, and conferences. He is also the founder of Full Cast Audio, an audiobook publishing company devoted to producing multivoiced recordings for family listening.

Like Nina Tanleven, Bruce Coville lives in Syracuse, New York. Unlike Nina, he is married and lives with his wife (and frequent collaborator), children's book illustrator Katherine Coville. Bruce and Katherine have three children, all of whom are now grown. They also play host to several cats, who have consented to let the Covilles feed and groom them.